THE HARD-BOILED VIRGIN

BROWN THRASHER BOOKS
The University of Georgia Press
ATHENS & LONDON

THE HARD-BOILED VIRGIN

FRANCES NEWMAN

FOREWORD BY

ANNE FIROR SCOTT

Published in 1993 as a Brown Thrasher Book
by the University of Georgia Press, Athens, Georgia 30602

Printed in the United States of America

97 96 95 94 93 P 5 4 3 2 1

Library of Congress Cataloging in Publication Data

Newman, Frances, d. 1928.
The hard-boiled virgin.
"Brown Thrasher Books."
Reprint of the 1926 ed. published by
Boni & Liveright, New York;
with a new foreword by A. F. Scott.
Includes bibliographical references.
I. Title.
[PZ3.N464Har 1980]
[PS3527.E883] 813'.52 80-16376
ISBN 0-8203-0526-X

FOREWORD

FRANCES NEWMAN, like the heroine of this novel, saw herself as "born to enjoy a small circulation among human beings," and she was right. She had enthusiastic admirers—James Branch Cabell, for example, called *The Hard-Boiled Virgin* a "shining, minor masterpiece" and said that if Newman had lived she would have become foremost among American women writers—but her fame was brief and insubstantial. The ponderous *Literary History of the United States* does not mention her name, nor do most of the historians and critics of early twentieth century literature.

In the southern literary renaissance, she stands in time somewhere between Amélie Rives, Ellen Glasgow, and Mary Johnston, all born a decade or more before her, and William Faulkner, Caroline Gordon, Thomas Wolfe, Katherine Anne Porter, Robert Penn Warren, and Eudora Welty, all born more than a decade after. She had more in common with the latter than the former, but in many ways she stands alone.

No one has yet written a biography of this southern lady who, like her heroine Katharine Faraday, was in revolt against all the dogmas that defined southern ladies. To reconstruct her life story, therefore, it is necessary to piece together the fragmentary recollections of the people who knew her. The only readily available primary source is an unsatisfactory edition of selected letters, published a year after her death. Her critical writing has never been collected. If it were ever brought together her place in the literary history of the twenties and the quality of her mind might be more sharply defined.

There is, of course, the fiction itself. She once advised a younger writer to "put in your own innermost emotions which are all any of us have to give to the world," and clearly there is something of Frances Newman in Katharine Faraday as well as in Isabel Ramsay of her second novel, *Dead Lovers Are Faithful Lovers.* In 1926 when *The Hard-Boiled Virgin* was just out, Newman complained that Atlanta was "shocked almost into convulsions" by the book, and that people were assuming that she had done everything in it. She deprecated that idea; nevertheless there are many similarities between her life and that of her heroine.

Frances Newman, like Katherine Faraday, was the last-born child in what southerners were accustomed to label a "distinguished" family, which is to say that her father was a Confederate veteran and a federal judge and her mother was descended from a man who had run for president. Like her heroine she was a dark, homely child in a family of beautiful blond sisters.

In a society that prefers women to be beautiful, homely girls take refuge, if they can, in the life of the mind, or they retreat into the arts. Newman, who said that Katharine had "brought herself up," developed at an early age a passion for reading and for showing off her precocious erudition, and she was also deeply interested in music. She began to write a novel at the age of ten, but stopped abruptly when she overheard a sister's beau making fun of some chapters she had unwisely left on a library table.

She balanced a miscellaneous school experience with rigorous self-education. Cabell said she was "at home in seven literatures," and esoteric allusions in her work bear him out. So far as we know, no other woman growing up in Atlanta in the nineties set herself to make scholarship, criticism, and fiction a serious career.

A strong urge to overcome provincialism led her to Europe twice before 1914. Between trips she studied Greek and Italian and library science. She said she became a librarian because she liked books (she quickly discovered this to be a naive view of what librarians do). After a year working at the Florida State College for Women, she joined the staff of the Carnegie Library in Atlanta, for whose bulletin she wrote the first of the penetrating book reviews that caught the eyes of Cabell and H. L. Mencken. They in turn introduced her to other writers, critics, and editors, including Emily Clark, whose Richmond literary magazine *The Reviewer* published some of her early work.

Atlanta, which she depicted with caustic irony, seems to have been her natural habitat, for though she tried writing in New York,

Paris, and the McDowell Colony, in the end she always came back to Georgia. During the First World War she published a good deal of literary journalism, first in the *Atlanta Constitution* and then in the *Atlanta Journal Sunday Magazine,* sometimes using the *nom de plume* Elizabeth Bennett in honor of Jane Austen.

Newman's criticism made few friends. Her literary standards were high and highly personal, and not many writers past or present compelled her admiration. In 1921 she published a series of complex critical pieces in *The Reviewer* in which she found almost every other writer in the world wanting—Compton MacKenzie, John Donald Wade, and Paul Morand were exceptions. Her harsh review of *This Side of Paradise* inspired F. Scott Fitzgerald to write what he described as the first letter he had ever addressed to a critic of his work. Others of her targets simply waited an opportunity to exact a literary eye for an eye. "She acquired enemies," Cabell wrote after her death, "with a pertinacity and a large unreason which I have not before nor since observed in any other human living."

Frances Newman would have been eccentric

anywhere; in Atlanta she seemed from another planet. Dressed always in shades of purple (unless she was in mourning), she chose her note-paper, sheets, and furniture also in lavender or lilac. She generally found life incomplete without a lover. In 1925 she reported a love affair, saying to a correspondent, "of course, it won't last, but love doesn't last, so it doesn't matter." Apparently it *didn't* last, since in 1926 she noted that she had not yet begun a new romance, but by 1927 she was able to write Cabell that that error had been repaired. A year later she told yet another correspondent that "a woman can't write a book without a father for it anymore than she could have a baby." Some of the men she chose to fall in love with were half her age, and of her published letters, a high proportion of those written in her forties were to three young men in their twenties. She said once that she would have liked to try marriage, briefly, to see how it would feel, but she never got around to it. Her household, after her mother's death in 1922, included her black "mammy" and an orphaned nephew she had raised and educated; she was deeply and sentimentally attached to both of them.

In 1924 she won an O. Henry Memorial Prize for a clever short story originally published in Mencken's *American Mercury*. "Rachel and Her Children" foreshadowed, both in theme and style, characteristics that would be more elaborately developed in later works.

Also in 1924 came her first book, *The Short Story's Mutations*, a scholarly *tour de force* that traced, with examples, the evolution of the short story from Petronius to Paul Morand, a contemporary French writer whom she greatly admired. A laconic line in the acknowledgments noted that "The English versions of stories from foreign languages are in all cases by Miss Newman." These included stories from Greek, Latin, French, Italian, and Danish. The book was thoroughly idiosyncratic and so erudite that only the most curious or most learned readers could have made much headway. Yet there was a second printing shortly after publication, and the book was widely reviewed. One critic, Elmer Davis, thought that reading it was "an enterprise as arduous as the pursuit of the Holy Grail, though somewhat more adequately rewarded."

As a consequence of the publication of *The*

Short Story's Mutations, Henry Seidel Canby invited Frances Newman to write a lead article in 1925 for the infant *Saturday Review of Literature*. She did so under the title "A Literary Declaration of Independence" and managed to insult nearly every living American writer and a few who were dead. By this time she was also writing reviews for the *Herald Tribune* and various New York journals.

Two years later, after a summer's residence at the McDowell Colony during which she made friends, among others, with Thornton Wilder and Hudson Strode, she finished *The Hard-Boiled Virgin*. Now it was her turn to be reviewed. She was fairly well pleased with Elmer Davis, who, after saying that she had done her best to spare herself the indignity of a large public, and after complaining about the title, the absence of either dialogue or paragraphs, and her complex style, concluded that for those sturdy enough to stay the course the trip was worth its price. Rebecca West, to Newman's fury, concluded that the book was not a work of art: "The miracle doesn't happen." The *Boston Transcript* thought it a "mental gymnastic" and the reviewer in the

New Republic was impatient: "How can this woman of rapier wit seriously believe there is anything clever about her affectedly cumbersome sentences?"

With the advantage of having been banned in Boston, the book sold briskly and went into a fifth printing two months after publication. In Atlanta it was the talk of that part of the town that read books, and caused a considerable scandal. No wonder, since every line was, in Elmer Davis's words, "grounds for lynching, unless Georgia and the South at large have lost their pristine vigor."

Meantime Newman herself, who did not mind at all that the book was making money, dickered about the sale of movie rights and reported that another novel was "fermenting nicely in my brain." A trip to Europe promoted the fermentation, and by the summer of 1927 she was once again at the McDowell Colony at work on the novel that became *Dead Lovers Are Faithful Lovers.* In January 1928 its manuscript went to the publisher; in April Newman left for France, partly, it would seem, to put some distance between herself and the reviews. Royalties from her first novel and an advance for the second, along with some skillful cajoling of the French Line (she promised to write about the beauties of the *Ile de France* in her newpaper column) allowed her to travel in unaccustomed luxury. Once in Paris she divided her time between serious scholarship—she was engaged in translating six stories of Jules LaForgue which Horace Liveright had agreed to publish—and a clothes-buying spree that made her a very model of French couturier splendor. Her book was known in France, reporters rushed to interview her, and she enjoyed life in Paris more than ever before. She had a dozen ideas for books and stories.

There were a few indications that success was mellowing her, but if so the world was never to know it. She developed a mysterious eye ailment that baffled first the French doctors, and then the American doctors whom she came home to consult. After a period of heroic effort during which, forbidden to use her eyes, she dictated the LaForgue translations as well as an introduction for them, she went to New York to visit one more famous doctor—and died. *Six Moral Tales from Jules LaForgue* were published almost at once, and a year later Hansell Baugh's edition of her letters appeared. Thereafter Frances Newman was seldom mentioned.

Why, more than half a century later, when her name is hardly recognized even by serious students of southern literature, is there now a new edition of *The Hard-Boiled Virgin*? Perhaps—and this would grieve Frances Newman—the reason is not principally literary. Newman was not a failed artist, but she was on a highly individual track. Her vision of a novel in which there would be "no dialog, no immediate scene, nothing at all but a diffused and purely subjective impression" was very much like that of Virginia Woolf, who was her exact contemporary. Possibly if she had lived, she would have achieved a masterpiece on the order of *To the Lighthouse*. As it is, her novels, though they are meticulously crafted, and filled with brilliant insights, require intense concentration of the reader who may, in the end, decide the effort was not worth it.

The late twentieth century reader is more likely to respond to the social insight of the novel, though aesthetic pleasure may indeed be a fringe benefit. There are intriguing sentences, for example, which hint at her sensitivity to the immorality of race relations in Georgia and which give point to a letter she wrote to a young columnist on the *Macon Telegraph* who proposed to include her in an article about literary rebels in Georgia: "So far as I know myself, I should say my interests are too literary, too concerned with style and form to make a very good rebel. But, when I think of the article I mean to write concerning the effect of the negro on the southern mind, I rather think that I must be one."

The central perspective of *The Hard-Boiled Virgin* which stands out clearly after half a century is its pervasive and corrosive feminism. It might amuse Newman to hear herself called a feminist—she who loved men and satirized women and who never carried a suffrage banner or talked about her rights—yet she was one of a very special and important kind. Beginning with "Rachel and Her Children," and continuing in both novels, she used irony to cut away the foundations of an edifice. That edifice was the pattern of upper-class southern urban life, especially the relations between men and women, a way of behaving which mistook form for substance, typified by the man in this book whose "confidence in the faith of his fathers which concerned God and women and negroes and cotton" made him impossible to talk to or listen to.

Probably the people best equipped to enjoy the glittering irony of this novel are southern women born before 1925 who can still remember the last stages of the social world Newman etched in acid, that world in which southern women were imprisoned in a fine web of expectations that it was almost death to defy.

Without a direct word about women's rights or sexual stereotypes, Newman's precise, mannered descriptions of southern social dogma made operational, of the marriage market, of the debutante racket, of the world as seen through the eyes of a precocious girl who wanted to kiss her elbow and who, by page 30, had already noticed that "any boy is born to a more honorable social situation than any girl," created a fine description of woman's condition. "I do think it is the first novel in which a woman ever told the truth about how women feel," she had written her publisher. And, later,

"I think women ordinarily will get a feeling men won't get." Isabel Paterson, reviewing *Dead Lovers* in the *Herald Tribune*, remarked of that book that "Most men will be unable to read it. It says a good many of the things men have tried by every social and economic device to avoid hearing."

Only an occasional reviewer of *The Hard-Boiled Virgin* observed its preoccupation with woman's condition, and none of her friends seem to have understood that her disgust with woman's place sometimes led her to disdain for the kind of women who were shaped by the confining web of social custom. Emily Clark noted Newman's "never failing well-spring of malice which created no illusions as to one's own ultimate fate with her," and went on to say: "Brilliant and acutely critical as she undoubtedly was, she, on occasion, saw quite commonplace persons in an apocalyptic light, in a fabulous region far beyond all criticism. These persons, however, were never women."

But was this malice to be understood in part as a reaction to her insights? A homely child in a culture that thought women ought to be beautiful, a determined intellectual in a society that thought women should have no mind: who was better equipped to be acutely aware of woman's deprivation? Katharine Faraday's reflections upon southern women's education on page 58 are illuminating: "if she had been sent across Peachtree Street to the Misses Rutherford's School, her brain would have been extracted in the process which the Misses Rutherford felt their duty to southern womanhood required, but that the remaining Miss Washington had felt her duty ended when she left the brains of her young ladies in a state of paralysis."

The whole book can be read as narrow but trenchant and persistent social criticism. It is as good an account as we are ever likely to have of the world young women of Newman's social station encountered as they grew up in the first decades of this century. It seems a safe guess that its reprinting will start a small Newman revival.

ANNE FIROR SCOTT

To
Frances Percy Alexander Newman,
the charming lady who gave me a
great deal more than
her name

THE HARD-BOILED VIRGIN

THE HARD-BOILED VIRGIN

THOUGH her father and mother would not have accounted for her in just that way, Katharine Faraday was the sixth pledge of their love. They had not much curiosity concerning the stars or the arts, and they would have been as unlikely to say that she was born under the sign of Virgo and in the earlier Beardsley period. But when she was eight years old, the spirit of that age was still unknown in cities far more worldly wise than Atlanta. The prestige of double beds and double standards was not seriously diminished, and society still called upon husbands to be as faithful as nature requires to tangent wives neatly buttoned into white cambric which flowed to their ankles, and upon wives to be as faithful as nature required to tangent husbands buttoned into white cambric which flowed only to their knees. Katharine Faraday's mother had no reason for suspecting that the Atlantic Ocean and the German language were concealing the opinions of Sigmund Freud from Georgia, or for suspecting that some women can be mothers only by day and wives only by night, and when Katharine Faraday had a sore throat which would almost certainly become measles before the next morning, her little walnut bed was moved into the carefully curtained off bay-window of her mother's room. But if Katharine Faraday had dared to risk escaping over its creaking rail, she would not have been lying in her bed when morning came, and her ears would not have been vainly stopped against her mother's reproaches and against her father's stumbling steps and his stumbling excuses. She did not like to feel the emotion she did not know was called pity, and she did not understand how her father could have reached such age and such eminence without learning that all mothers are as infallible as any pope and more righteous than any saint. Neither did she understand why he had never learned that wise husbands and children acknowledge their sins immediately, and acknowledge them with such despair and such moving lamentations that virtue is likely to relent, and that unless she relents she finds herself unable to compete with the repentant sinner's self-abasement. She had already discovered the awkwardness of quarrels between partners of a bed, but if she had known that she was beginning to walk in the holy footprints of Saint Katharine of Alexandria, she could not have wept longer when she discovered that the horrifying felicities of the holy bonds of matrimony sometimes follow the horrors of connubial fury, and when she discovered that a father and a mother are a man and a woman—that they are not only one flesh, but two.

George and Marian Faraday were so beautifully brought up that they never had any ideas more unusual than the ideas of Peachtree Street, on which they were born. Eleanor and Arthur Faraday were no more than nicely brought up, but they were always able to take the serious view of the Piedmont Driving Club's importance which made Eleanor Faraday a satisfactory partner for its most fashionable members. But Alex and Katharine Faraday were not brought up at all, except when they risked a crime so noisy that it reached the ears of a mother absorbed by two daughters who had attained every social honour except marriage. They were escorted to the correct kindergarten when they reached the age of four and to the correct schools when they reached the age of six. But they began their education in a room which had some reason for being called a library, and since their mother still proclaimed her elegant adherence to the vanishing law which allowed well-bred young ladies no tributes except flowers and books and chocolates, Katharine Faraday passed from The Tar Baby and The Ugly Duckling and Alice to The Happy Prince and The Happy Hypocrite and The Dolly Dialogues, and to the tale of Cupid and Psyche in the cool violet twilight of Walter Pater's prose. When the history of the little mermaid, whom love and a cruel sea-witch transformed into the saddest heroine of fairyland, allowed the inference that happiness ever after is not the invariable consequence of feminine love in Scandinavia or even in fairyland, Katharine Faraday was consoled by the history of Lord George Hell, whom Mr. Beerbohm and love and a wax mask transformed into Lord George Heaven—beside the more gracious banks of the Serpentine. Mr. Beerbohm and Mr. Wilde and Sir Anthony Hope Hawkins made her hopelessly Anglomanic before she was ten years old, and they gave her a taste for the Oxford manner which made the literature of her own country unbearable to her, and which drove her to the consistency of abandoning a heroine called Violet Carewe in the middle of a chapter called Deeper Depths, when she realized that her own novel must necessarily be an American novel.

The inevitability of her literary nationality was almost as great a sorrow to Katharine Faraday as her unprofitable efforts to kiss her sharp elbows. But when she was already too old to plead youthful irresponsibility in a hell which had been showering brimstone on infants less than a span long for three hundred years, a frightful immortality was revealed to her by a story called Elsie Dinsmore and a play called Doctor Faustus, and her childhood was darkened by the impossibility of getting rid of a deathless soul almost certainly predestined to hell. She was not born a mystic, but merely human reason could hardly have been responsible for her conviction that her troublesome soul—like other people's—was the shape of a cantaloupe seed and nearly the same colour, and that it was about ten inches long, and that it was made of a translucent cartilaginous substance with a small oval bone in the centre. She thought that its salvation would have been easy enough if she had been asked to walk through actual Sloughs of Despond and past merely physical Apollyons, but although she had heard that she was a child of the covenant, this curious new birth was even more mysterious to her than balance on a bicycle or dead weight on a piano. Since she had been denied the convincing raptures which heaven had granted to her mammy and to Elsie Dinsmore and to Saint Paul, and since her natural confidence in a printed page had been greatly increased by her observation that little girls whose hair is black and straight should be more erudite than little girls whose hair is fair and curly, she set herself to search the scriptures. But after the first chapter of the prophecy of Isaiah, she abandoned her oval soul to its fate, and she abandoned it with a relief as great as the relief she was destined to feel when she abandoned John Ruskin after his first morning in Florence, and Samuel Johnson after his first cup of tea, and all the other major and minor prophets in their turn —whether they were inspired from Sinai or from Parnassus.

Katharine Faraday's mother had heard in her cradle that a nation which could prefer a Lincoln to a Breckenridge was unlikely to return to the conviction that elegance is the greatest of human virtues, and she had even heard delicate suggestions that a God who could look down unmoved on the triumph of a Grant over a Lee could hardly expect to be acquitted of increasingly democratic sympathies. But until Marian Faraday was entering on her third season as the inevitable choice of every cotillion's leader, and Eleanor Faraday was entering on her second season as her city's official beauty, she was not able to share her husband's conviction that Alex Faraday would probably find more clients and more constituents in the school which his city provided for nothing at all than in the school which Dr. Gordon provided for two hundred dollars a year. And until Marian Faraday's waltzing was inspiring orchestra leaders for the fifth season and Eleanor Faraday's beauty was adorning the box-seat of coaches for the fourth season, her mother did not decide to convince her father that Katharine Faraday's peculiarities would be more likely to succumb to the rigidities of the Calhoun Street School than to the leniencies of the Misses Washington's School. Marian Faraday went down to New Orleans and led a figure of the Carnival German in one of the gowns her father's acquiescence provided, and Eleanor Faraday wore the other gown when she went to supper at the first Richmond German on the arm of its most marriageable member. But if Katharine Faraday had ever heard of a writer called George Meredith, and if she had known that she was not created to enjoy a wider circulation among human beings than his novels enjoyed, her peculiarities would hardly have been lessened by learning her destiny from a little girl whose divine commission had no external symbols except an aquiline nose, a crimson crêpe de chine frock pleated like an accordion, and the carefully curled hair of an oldest daughter. Ten years afterwards, when Katharine Faraday read the last chapter of a book called Stover at Yale, and suffered with its hero the agonies which are voluntarily endured by every young gentleman who survives until the third Thursday of his third May at Yale, she suffered again from the memory of the day when a line of submissive children stood on the red clay of the Calhoun Street School's yard and waited for the tap which was also an accolade, and which settled their eligibility for a game called Prisoner's Base as publicly as his belated tap settled Stover's eligibility for a society called Skull and Bones. And she realized that the thousands of young gentlemen who had walked untapped from the shadow of that historic oak were very unlike the little girl who was dressed in a dark green frock which abbreviation had not precisely adapted to her, and who walked away from the line of children before fate could reveal to them that she had wanted something which fate might not intend to give her.

At the age of twelve, Katharine Faraday could not be expected to know what a great many celebrated novelists and a great many celebrated dramatists have died without learning, and when she left the row of expectant heads and walked across the hard red clay yard to pick up a rusty dipper, she did not suspect that character was condescending to allow chance its usual small share in the union which becomes fate. She did not like the rust-flavoured water, but she drank three dippers of it so slowly that she dispatched nearly five minutes of the long half hour she must destroy with dignity before she could go back to the easy triumphs of spelling and of mental arithmetic. She drank them under the eyes of a little girl who had been brought to the necessity of drinking water by the discovery that a girl who had been born a Rutledge, and whose mother had been born a Rhett, might travel one night's journey from the city of Charleston, and that she might then suffer the suggestion of being left untapped by a child who would never be allowed to dance, or to eat terrapin, or to drink champagne at a Saint Cecilia Ball, and who would never walk up the middle aisle of Saint Michael's Church and be married to a Middleton or a Pringle or a Pinckney. Sarah Rutledge could not believe in the existence of towns where personal charms, including frocks and houses and even brains, were more useful than ancestors who had signed their names to a document called The Declaration of Independence. But since she had heard that Katharine Faraday's father was a person of some consequence, she was willing to sit down on a bench beside her, and to discuss this strange new idea with her, and to eat one of her beaten biscuits. Sarah Rutledge had no biscuits, but she was the oldest of six daughters, and she had information which the youngest of three daughters and three sons had easily lived twelve years without acquiring. As a courteous return for the biscuit, she told Katharine Faraday all she knew concerning the birth of Harriet Rutledge, who had come into the world just in time to escape the disgrace of being born off the soil of South Carolina. She dwelt with satisfaction on the dreadful sounds which had come through the opening and closing door of her mother's room, and Katharine Faraday listened with attention and even with interest, but she did not find that the Charlestonian accent conveyed the impression of great intelligence, and since she had no doubt that the arrival of a sixth daughter would wring shrieks from her own self-possessed mother, she decided that babies issuing from their mothers were at least as improbable as golden gowns issuing from hazel-nuts or genii issuing from lamps. But she was not very happy, and she realized that the possession of one intimate friend is the most dignified barrier against the possible neglect of society—and particularly the possession of an intimate friend whose lineage entitled her to marriage with a Middleton or a Pringle or a Pinckney, and to a wedding in Saint Michael's Church. Katharine Faraday had an excellent memory, and when Eleanor Faraday had gone over for the second Saint Cecilia Ball the winter before, her mother had spoken several times of the advantages and disadvantages of marriage with the Middletons and the Pinckneys.

The more carefully curled little girls, and the little boys who wore comparatively unspotted blue serge, usually walked towards the west when they left the Calhoun Street School, but Katharine Faraday walked a block towards the south before she walked a block towards the west. She was glad no very important children walked with her, because important children always seemed to be oldest sons and oldest daughters, and they would not have been likely to understand why she had directions to come into the house by its side door, and to hang her hat and her coat in the dark closet under the oak stairs, and to be sure there were no guests before she came into the dining room. Even if she had not been warned into silence in the morning, she knew there would probably be guests whenever either Marian or Eleanor Faraday had been to a dance with a young gentleman whose bouquet would certainly be large enough and durable enough to decorate a table the next day, and when a gentleman who was anxious to incur obligations had chosen that week as a useful time to send their father a barrel of oysters or a dozen birds or a wild turkey. But she did not know that there were guests so often because, although Marian and Eleanor Faraday understood that invitations from men are vastly more desirable than invitations from women, they also understood the advisability of giving lunches for girls who were staying with important girls and for girls who lived in important towns, and she did not know that their lunches—like other people's, and like the oysters and the birds and the turkeys—were given for the purpose of incurring obligations oftener than they were given for the purpose of paying them off. If she opened the side door to a quality of laughter and a volume of conversation her family never produced in private, she slipped into the library and through the back hall into the pantry, where she could enjoy whatever birds' legs and cheese balls and charlotte russe the guests left for her to enjoy. And then, since the town of Atlanta still took its lunch and dinner guests into the bedroom it admired most,

Katharine Faraday always took her schoolbooks from the pantry to the attic, where only a burst of ascending laughter could tell her that her sisters' guests were walking up the oak stairs to collect their carefully fitted coats from the best bedspreads, and to assure themselves that the plumes and the aigrettes on their large black velvet hats were sweeping towards their right shoulders at the correct angle. The same nervous temperament which distracted her if she left home less than half an hour before school began, and the same pride of intellect which made her read the plays of William Shakespeare and Christopher Marlowe, made her begin by working out her problems in principal and interest, according to a rule she did not understand. When she had written her name on the papers whose absence would have been so much more dangerous than the absence of invisible information, she read over a description of the Battle of Lexington or the Battle of Chickamauga or the Battle of Santiago—none of which she suspected of being overestimated—and then she ran her eyes down three columns of words she had already met in the works of the great

Victorians—none of whom she suspected of being overestimated. After that, if the carefully fitted coats were still lying on the best bedspreads and their owners were still drinking coffee and crême de menthe, and still discussing The Girl of the Golden West and The Sultan of Sulu and designs for petticoat ruffles and for white satin blouses and the fate of the latest of the defaulters who had bought bouquets for them, she looked at the piles of magazines her father was certainly going to have bound some day. In one pile of them she read a story which was called Trilby, and which had been written by an Englishman called George Du Maurier. She disapproved of it because the hero's mother persuaded him to forsake a tall and lovely heroine merely because she was a laundress, but she liked it better than a story by another Englishman who was called Hardy and who did not write any better than if he had been an American, and of which she remembered only that it was called Hearts Insurgent and that its hero and heroine killed a pig. Sometimes she passed over her father's orderly piles for the large flat magazines Marian Faraday was going to cut up for scrapbooks some day. She looked at pictures of rooms as they should not be and at pictures of rooms as they should be, and she saw very little difference between them. She read a great many pages of advice to girls, and she saw only what she had already heard and what she had no reason not to believe—that no girl can allow any man to touch so much as her pocket handkerchief until he has humbly begged her to become his wife, and that she cannot allow him to touch anything very much more intimate than her pocket handkerchief until she has become his wife. On a Wednesday afternoon when the conversation was prolonged beyond the interest of all the large flat magazines—the conversation was about Laura Black's cleverness in getting Robert Inman back by the device of sending him a chocolate cake and untruthfully saying that she had made it for him herself, Katharine Faraday afterwards overheard—she opened a magazine which was called Lippincott's, and she began to read a story called A Marital Liability. She realized that it was an American novel, but she went on with the story of the honourable husband and his unworthy wife until she came to a discussion of the unworthy wife's affection for her daughter. And there she read that the affection was the result of something Miss Elizabeth Phipps Train called childbirth pains, and she remembered that when she had searched the scriptures she had read about women who were delivered of a child, and who remembered their anguish no more, for joy that a man was born into the world. She had supposed that Saint John was only continuing the mysterious threats which she had read in the books that the minister's daughter said were written by Moses, and which seemed to have no connection with the merely secular processes of nature. But she knew that an author so contemporary and so unlike even a minor prophet as Miss Elizabeth Phipps Train would not be likely to mention childbirth pains so casually unless there were such things as childbirth pains. And she knew that the birth of Harriet Rutledge must have been as uncomfortable for her mother as Sarah Rutledge thought it was, and that her own birth must have been as uncomfortable for her mother as Harriet Rutledge's birth was for Mrs. Pinckney Rutledge, and that when she had been taken to see an actress who was called Sarah Bernhardt and who would almost certainly be dead before Katharine Faraday could become old enough to appreciate her, the chairs in the skating-rink must have held thousands of people who had been born in the same way that Harriet Rutledge was born.

Even before Katharine Faraday observed that the stupidest girl with a short upper lip and curly golden hair is born to a social situation much pleasanter than the social situation of the cleverest girl with a long upper lip and straight black hair, she knew that any boy is born to a more honourable social situation than any girl. And after she had observed that a boy's honourable situation seemed to be the result of his inability to produce a baby rather than to his ability to produce an idea, she still went on saying that she was sorry she had not been able to make her thin lips touch one of her sharp elbows before she lost confidence in a kissed elbow's efficacy in changing a girl into a boy. She did not become reconciled to her own sex even after the Christmas morning when George Faraday fainted—apparently because his beautiful upbringing had not provided him with practice in drinking six glasses of champagne, and certainly when he was exchanging the garments in which he had spent the night for the garments in which he meant to spend the morning—just before the family processional was ready to go down and see her show the touching childish belief in Santa Claus's existence and the rapturous satisfaction with his gifts which she knew were the correct rewards of her father's bills and her mother's labours. She felt almost sure that her oldest brother could not be made in God's image, and that he must be suffering from something like the disease Mildred Cobb said was responsible for her Aunt Ellen's increasingly enormous nose, but she never again tried to kiss one of her sharp elbows. After George Faraday's return to consciousness and to correct covering made childish happiness suitable again, Katharine Faraday went down to her little pine-tree and played the pleasant part of a delighted child, but at ten o'clock her mother and her mammy had exchanged their conviction that Malaga grapes and venison steak were not a breakfast Katharine Faraday could cope with even once a year.

Katharine Faraday always thought that a bath in the morning was merely one part of the process of getting dressed, and no greater luxury than buttoning a tucked Fruit of the Loom petticoat to a slightly corrugated garment called an underbody, or guiding hair into two adequately long and adequately thick braids and then tying them tightly with two very dark brown satin ribbons which were supposed to match the hair they tied and which must be creased in the same places every morning and rolled up and pinned every night. Half a dozen years before, whenever her mother had put on the grey crêpe de chine with the brocaded panels or the violet crêpe de chine with the rose point yoke, and had gone out with her two older daughters to inspect the débutante daughters or the new daughters-in-law of her acquaintances, the afternoons had usually been occupied by baths surreptitiously shared with Alex Faraday and enlivened by soap-bubbles and by slides down the angular end of the tub—baths approved by a sympathetic mammy on the condition that Alex and Katharine Faraday would keep their backs turned towards each other. That was in the days when Katharine Faraday was just acquiring the art of reading, and before she discovered that even when she went out to call on other little girls, neither conversation nor paper dolls called Royal Reggie and Lordly Lionel were as reliable amusements as two books read on opposite sides of a room. But Katharine Faraday did not usually enjoy the books she read when her feet were on a lower level than her head. She considered her father's large leather chair exactly the right width for resting a head on one arm and the under side of knees on the other, but it was not often available in her leisure hours except on a few early afternoons and on Saturday mornings. And since the custom of paying calls was not yet extinct among the ladies and gentlemen of Atlanta, the white fur rug in the drawing-room was so exposed that she was obliged to slip behind the blue curtains every time the doorbell rang. She did not find any other reading room as luxuriously comfortable as a bath-room with its mirror and its window obliterated by steam, or any chair as luxuriously comfortable as a bath of water so hot that reproaches for drawing all the water out of the boiler were inevitable, or any other hour as luxuriously comfortable as the last hour before she got into her white iron bed. The hour before she went to bed was very often the hour before George and Eleanor and Marian Faraday went out to dance, but on a January evening when George and Marian and Eleanor Faraday were adding distinction to the Capital City Club's dinner-dance, and when Arthur Faraday was addressing the voters of the fifth ward, and Alex Faraday was trying to throw a round leather ball into the Georgia Military Academy's high basket, she slipped her left foot into water so hot that she remembered the immortality of her soul with terror. But the terror was noticeably slightly more than the pious terror she had suffered three years before, and she slipped herself joint by joint under the burning water before she opened a brown book called Sentimental Tommy and laid it on the wooden rim of the tub. Before she went on with the history of the afternoon when Tommy ran away with Grizel because Grizel would have ceased to be respectable if she had run away alone, she lay down to meditate serenely and to forget the play called Macbeth which was not a book to read in a pleasant place like a hot bath. She looked at the convex reflections of herself in the nicely polished faucets, and the reflections were both so unsatisfactory that she looked down at as much of herself as she could see. She saw that her chest seemed likely to remain flatter than Sarah Rutledge's, and much flatter than Mildred Cobb's, but she knew that her sisters never went out of the house without ruffles inside their blouses, and that in spite of the necessity for ruffles they had more admirers and more desirable admirers than Mildred Cobb's youngest aunt. She also saw that her legs were very thin and very straight, but she had been told that time would certainly enlarge them, and that it might even curve them. Between her flat chest and her thin legs, she noticed a line she had never noticed before—a delicate line which was slightly browner than the area she thought was her stomach, and which began just below the curious little dent her mammy called a navel. And she had a sudden revelation that when her first child—of whose advent she had so little doubt that she had already baptized her Violet, with Diana reserved for her younger sister—came into the world, the part of herself which she thought was her stomach would burst along the delicate brown line, and that she would naturally shriek, and that her daughter would dart into the world like Pallas Athena darting from the brain of Zeus, and that a doctor would then give her ether and sew her up. In the light of the revelation, she could see why a doctor was in a house whenever a baby was born there, and that if nature had only provided prospective mothers with some way of foreseeing when a child was likely to be born and of having the ether before the line burst, all discomfort could easily have been avoided. Katharine Faraday jumped out of the bath she had intended to enjoy as long as the hot water in the boiler held out, and before she was quite dry, she had covered herself with a Fruit of the Loom nightgown. She took up her brown book, but she covered herself with a sheet and two pairs of blankets and an eiderdown comfort before she went on with the difficulties of the little boy whose conduct seemed so entirely reasonable to her.

Katharine Faraday's world was enough like the great world to believe that the people who are most elegantly established in this world will certainly be most elegantly established in the world to come, and to believe that dining and dancing at the Capital City Club on Saturday evening was the only correct preparation for singing and praying at Saint Luke's Protestant Episcopal Church or at the First Presbyterian Church on Sunday morning. And Katharine Faraday was so much like the rest of her world that even before she gave up hope of saving her soul, she began to neglect her International Sunday School Quarterly long enough to spend the earlier hours of her Saturday evenings in the blue room on whose outer door she often read the announcement that Marian and Eleanor Faraday would have eight guests for lunch. When she watched Marian Faraday settle the Roman waves of her yellow-gold hair and coil it into a Psyche knot above her classic profile, Katharine Faraday looked with mortification at the straight black braids of her own hair. When Eleanor Faraday slipped her union suit off her celebrated shoulders and smoothly folded its long sleeves around the top of her long, hard, white corset, she remembered with mortification that her own chest and her own waist and her own hips had almost exactly the same circumference. And when Eleanor Faraday buttoned her scalloped white flannel petticoat and hooked her ruffled white taffeta petticoat, and stepped on a sheet and then carefully slipped a trailing green satin gown over her smoothly parted red-gold hair, Katharine Faraday looked with mortification at the dark green wool sleeves which ended around her own chapped brown wrists. But she gathered from their conversation that she would find an evening at the Capital City Club even more unpleasant than a morning at the First Presbyterian Church, and she did not want to dance there until her nineteenth birthday made dances inevitable. She was sure that she would find dances a good deal more painful than recess at the Calhoun Street School, and that the suspense of waiting for a partner who would make her eligible for the next favour at a cotillion would be almost unbearable to a girl who had not been able to wait for a tap which would have made her eligible to play Prisoners' Base. When a ring at the door had announced the arrival of a carriage called a landau and of two members of the Capital City Club, and when Marian and Eleanor Faraday had slipped on their fur-edged black carriage shoes for themselves and picked up the fur-edged blue and green capes the two members of the Capital City Club would drape around their shoulders, Katharine Faraday went back to her own room. But instead of opening the International Sunday School Quarterly, she slipped off her green checked dress and her white Fruit of the Loom petticoat and her union suit, and then she looked at her high forehead and her straight nose and her long upper lip in the mirror over the walnut chest of drawers she called a bureau. On the evening when she opened The Girls' Book of Famous Queens at a drawing of Cleopatra, Queen of Egypt, she took up a yellow silk blanket which Marian Faraday had bought in Naples and which had been washed so often that it had descended from her wide mahogany bed to Katharine Faraday's white iron bed. She draped the yellow blanket around her thin shoulders and drew it tightly around her body's only curve and pinned it with two carefully concealed safety pins, and then she looked at her walnut-framed glass portrait. She had never doubted the accuracy of the judgments she read in the newspapers and in her school-books, and she remembered the photograph of the Historian General of the Georgia Daughters of the Confederacy which she had seen in the Atlanta Constitution, and the lines concerning the Historian General's brilliant mind which were printed under the photograph. And she remembered the photograph of an author who was called George Eliot, and the paragraphs concerning her brilliant mind which were printed in the front of a book called The Mill on the Floss, and she could not believe there was any really good reason why no one had ever told her that she was surprisingly pretty for a girl who was as clever as she was.

When Katharine Faraday was twenty-one years old and was privileged to see the schoolrooms of Oxford and Cambridge, and to read the first volume of a story called Sinister Street which had just been written by an Oxonian called Compton Mackenzie, she remembered that every room in the Calhoun Street School was long and wide and high and ugly in exactly the same way the other seven rooms were, and she began to suspect that the prose of her own country might be due to the difference between whitewashed walls and panelled oak walls. But when she was thirteen years old, she did not suspect that whitewashed schoolrooms might finally justify her decision not to increase the number of American novels, and she was not much concerned with any of her schoolroom's ugly details except the square blackboard between its two back windows. Since no little boy would have considered admitting that he could draw roses and violets and carnations, some gifted little girl adorned the square blackboard with a wreath of those flowers on the first day of every month, and portrayed each of them in the chalk which seemed to her most nearly like its natural colour. Inside the wreath, she wrote the names of her fellow students whom examination was supposed to have proved ignorant of less than five per cent of the truths and conjectures they had enjoyed the opportunity of learning during the month which had just ended. The list was called The Roll of Honour, and its attainment called with it the practical privilege of choosing a seat for the month. But when Katharine Faraday was thirteen years old, little girls were still denied the satisfaction of dreaming about the day when they would walk up the broad steps of the capitol at Washington, and there take an oath to defend the Constitution of the United States. And in all the eight rooms of the Calhoun Street School, little girls were denied the satisfaction of sitting in the first seat of the first row of desks, even when their names were written high above the name of any little boy, and when Katharine Faraday's name was first written just under the spray of maidenhair fern which marked the zenith of the wreath, she was obliged to choose the first seat of the second row of desks. That seat carried with it the honour of leading the line of girls out of the room and down the stairs at eleven o'clock and at two, of feeling too tall and too awkward and too important when she collected the examination papers of her row, and when she carried the wicker waste-paper basket down the aisle between the desirable first and second rows, up the aisle between the acceptable third and fourth rows, and down the aisle between the outcast fifth and sixth rows. But the boy who sat across the aisle from her, in the seat he did not owe entirely to his scholarship, had all those honours except the honour of carrying the waste-paper basket, and he also had the incomparably greater honour of opening half the door every time he was able to think he heard a knock, and of throwing open both its halves at eleven o'clock and two. Katharine Faraday did not know all the differences there are between boys and girls, and she did not suspect that a boy who would choose to sit in the front of a schoolroom, even for the honour of opening a double door, would never write good prose or compose good music or paint good pictures, and that he was unlikely even to succeed in cutting out an appendix or in leading an army, and she was taken with a romantic attachment for him which she did not doubt was love. She found him interesting because he sat opposite her and she corrected his papers and saw his figures and his letters every day, and because his mother was dead and his name was Cary Fairfax. But she was taken with the romantic attachment on the day when he put an iron ring around his ear and then smiled at her, and because he was one of those favoured beings who are not created to produce babies and who, consequently, can sit in the first row of desks without being as clever as she thought that she was, and who can become president of the United States without being as clever as she intended to become. And though she was much more interested in her own emotions than she was in his emotions, she did not try to discover the reasons why she had suddenly begun to find him almost as interesting as she found herself, and if she had tried, she would not have been likely to discover that she did not have any reasons. But she had often heard that little boys are a good deal like grown men, and that they are not usually taken with romantic attachments for little girls who can spell words of five syllables and who can find the eighteenth term of an arithmetical progression. She did not want to discover that he suspected her of an attachment he had not invited her to conceive, and even when she met him under the amorous influence of a party and of Saint Valentine's Day and of a game called Clap in and Clap out, she did not want him to offer her the indignity of a kiss. But when she was offered that indignity by a little boy whom she had never before seen outside the pious gloom of the First Presbyterian Church's Sunday School room, she was not sorry that Cary Fairfax saw the indignity offered her, or that he saw the expression of outraged virtue which she was not able to feel. She was sure the little boy from the Sunday school could not know how well informed she was about the kings of Israel and the kings of Judah and the journeys of Saint Paul, and she did not begin to wonder if little girls usually find favour in the sight of the little boys who have not found favour in their sight. And she did not regret that pride of intellect had triumphed over love that very morning, and that it had kept her from deciding to mistake the number of repetitions in the word assassinate on her own paper, and from deciding to overlook the definition of the word venerable on Cary Fairfax's paper.

Since Alex Faraday had gone into long trousers, the judgment of his peers did not allow him to admit publicly that he had a mother or a sister, and Katharine Faraday walked down Peachtree Street alone on the Sunday morning before Easter. Instead of considering the spiritual condition in which she would shortly partake of the Lord's Supper for the first time, she considered the possibility of meeting the boy who had wanted to smirch her virgin dignity with a kiss. He had curly hair and an upturned nose, which she considered destructive to his personal distinction. And she had been told that he went to the Ivy Street School, which convinced her that his father could not be a member of the Capital City Club or of the Piedmont Driving Club, and which strengthened a suspicion that had been growing since she had discovered her Sunday school's musical director in the act of repairing Mildred Cobb's furnace—a suspicion that membership in the First Presbyterian Church was not a complete social reference. She was almost sure that her first admirer would probably never be able to take her to a Cotillion or even to a Nine O'Clock German, and she was so depressed by the idea of becoming one of those girls who appeal to the wrong kind of men that when she crossed Marietta Street and met the boy's undiscouraged gaze, she suffered all the mortification Beatrice Portinari could have suffered when Dante Alighieri turned a tragic adoration towards her. She hurried down the steep granite steps which led to the gas-lit basement in which she had first heard of the light that is fairer than day and in which she had first had a public opportunity of displaying her excellent memory, and she hurried down the creaking yellow aisle into the protection of the minister's daughter, whom Protestant custom had ordained to the service of God at her conception, as it had ordained her mother at her marriage. But the Presbyterian Church had not given the minister's daughter instruction along with ordination, and Katharine Faraday's father did not converse with his children. And even if her mother had not been too much concerned with chafing-dishes and well-baked hams to give her youngest daughter instruction at her knee on Sunday evenings, and if she had not considered the discussion of religion on week-days as unbecoming a southern lady as affection for her husband, Katharine Faraday would still have sat beside the minister's daughter for the last time without ever having suspected that people ask the names of each other's religions for any other purpose than the establishment of their probable social importance. She would also have been received into the church of John Calvin without ever having heard of John Calvin, and although she might have heard that people who know the Westminster Shorter Catechism are too rational to build churches or to hold services which can possibly delight any one of the five human senses, she would not have been likely to hear that the First Presbyterian Church was a good deal less delightful to the eye than its builders had meant it to be. But she had a wider acquaintance with literature than she had with architecture, and she had observed that the stories in the Sunday school's library were very unlike the stories of Mr. Wilde and Mr. Pater, and she had observed that the Sunday school's superintendent apparently had not a complete knowledge of English grammar. She did not mention these observations to the minister's daughter, and she had never mentioned them to her father and mother, because she knew that southern ladies and gentlemen respect the polite fictions of society, and she was sure they must be silently aware that forgetting the names of the presidents of the United States and the emperors of Rome has mortifying consequences, but that forgetting the names of the kings of Judah and the whole Westminster Shorter Catechism apparently has no consequences at all. Her suspicions of the Sunday school's importance had not affected her respectful fear of the red brick church over it, and she did not doubt that the church was superior to the Sunday school—as superior as its red body Brussels carpet was to the strips of creaking yellow which covered the aisles between the Sunday school's yellow pine benches, and which she had always supposed was made of the substance called oakum that prisoners picked in the melancholy stories of those Englishmen who had not enjoyed the advantage of an Oxford education. But when Katharine Faraday left the minister's daughter and walked back up the steep granite steps and sat down in her father's walnut pew as a responsible member of the church, her reason could not support a minister who addressed an omniscient god in a discourse called a prayer, and then used it as an opportunity for telling his congregation the news of the week. And when his sermon omitted all explanation of the reasons why the Children of Israel settled on a golden calf as a cheeringly visible object of worship, she began to think that if she had not happened to see a picture of the goddess Hathor three days before, no one in his church would have known that the minister was at least one fact removed from omniscience. But she still did not understand why she had not fallen dead at the minister's feet when she had assured him and his inquiring elders that she believed Jesus Christ died on the cross so that she might have eternal life. Neither did she understand why she continued to live after she had swallowed a small piece of bread which looked a good deal like the bread her mother's cook called light bread, but which was now evidence that she believed Christ's body was broken for her, or why she was not struck down to the red carpet when she swallowed the correctly small sip of a wine which seemed to be a good deal like the port wine she always had when she was too thin, but which was now evidence that Christ's blood was shed for her. In spite of her satisfaction with her own cleverness and with her own knowledge that the goddess Hathor had horns, she lived six years longer before she was able to believe that she had been right and that all the rest of her world had been wrong.

Although Katharine Faraday knew that her chest was flatter than Sarah Rutledge's chest, and much flatter than Mildred Cobb's, she felt her defeat when Mildred Cobb was driven to the Calhoun Street School after a day's absence, and explained her absence with consciously reticent references to her mother's unwillingness to have her feet wet, which, Katharine Faraday realized even before the reticence ended, could only mean that Mildred Cobb had become a woman. And when Sarah Rutledge invited Katharine Faraday to picnic with Saint Luke's Sunday School beside a stream which was just the right depth for wading, and then refused to wade because her mother thought the water was likely to be too cold, Katharine Faraday recognized the same conscious reticence, and before it ended she realized that Sarah Rutledge had become a woman. But Sarah Rutledge was an oldest child and Mildred Cobb was an oldest daughter, and Katharine Faraday's mother did not lay down her comb when she received the announcement of an event which Katharine Faraday would have found alarming if her acquaintances had allowed her to live fifteen years in the state of innocence her mother thought good breeding required. She assured Katharine Faraday that the state of her health did not require the interruption of her education for even one morning, and she did not mention the possible consequences of wet feet. Since the day and the Misses Washington's garden were completely dry, Katharine Faraday was saved from the necessity of exaggerating her mother's concern, but she was obliged to abandon reticence sooner than either she or Mildred Cobb thought good breeding allowed. And since Mildred Cobb's forefathers had left their names to three of the more celebrated counties in the state of Georgia, and their blood on all the more celebrated southern battlefields, and since her father usually knew on Wednesday what the price of cotton would be on Thursday, she did not feel obliged to assume a polite interest which regular recurrence had naturally lessened, and Katharine Faraday was left with only the private satisfaction of her conviction that she would not disappoint the hope of her husband, or the hope of her husband's father and mother, when she married into a family so ancient that its dignity demanded an immediate heir.

When Katharine Faraday was fifteen years old and Marian Faraday had made a marriage which was more satisfactory to herself than it was to her mother or her father or her bridegroom—but which was entirely satisfactory to the young ladies whom she had been leading down the Capital City Club's ball-room for varying numbers of years, since it did not decrease the number of marriageable young gentlemen in their world—Katharine Faraday's mother had decided that the increasingly democratic sympathies of her god would not enter the sphere of women before Katharine Faraday was nineteen years old. And since the divine progress was so unhurried, she had decided that even the necessities of Eleanor Faraday's wardrobe must give way to the necessity of providing Katharine Faraday with several intimate friends whose great-grandfathers had given their names to the counties of the more distinguished southern states, whose fathers knew on Wednesday what the price of cotton would be on Thursday, whose brothers were members of the Piedmont Driving Club, and whose mothers would be arranging careful dinners and dances and lunches in another four years. The great-grandfathers and the announcements of the Misses Washington assured those virtues in every young lady who walked under the fanlight of their white door, and since public opinion assured them in a reasonable number of their young ladies, Katharine Faraday had abandoned the pursuit of knowledge, and she had gone back to the Misses Washington's School. She did not suspect that she had abandoned anything except the compact eloquence of a Roman called Cicero, and she was thirty years old before observation showed her that if she had been sent across Peachtree Street to the Misses Rutherford's School, her brain would have been extracted in the process which the Misses Rutherford felt their duty to southern womanhood required, but that the remaining Miss Washington had felt her duty ended when she left the brains of her young ladies in a state of paralysis. The young ladies whom Miss Washington was reducing to a mental state which was likely to make them satisfactory partners for the members of the Piedmont Driving Club were not the human beings among whom Katharine Faraday was destined to enjoy her small circulation. And when Eleanor Faraday made a marriage which was satisfactory to every one except the young ladies whom she had preceded up the ladders of coaches for varying numbers of years, Katharine Faraday's mother remembered that even though Hans Christian Andersen could hardly have understood polite society, he did not expect a duckling to become a swan in its own pond. The adequacy of Eleanor Faraday's hats and frocks and nightgowns and chemises convinced her mother that she could not send her youngest daughter so far away from her as Paris, or even so far as New York, and she decided that if Katharine Faraday went to Washington and observed the ladies of the diplomatic corps for two winters, she would come back to Atlanta with a more ingenious method of doing her hair and with some information concerning methods of rousing ardent but honourable passions in young gentlemen. During the seasonable month of January, Katharine Faraday began her observation of the ladies who had achieved marriage with ambassadors. But they did not often seem to remember the afternoons or the hours when they could call on the ladies who had achieved marriage with the senators and the congressmen who accurately represented the state of Georgia, and although she observed them in theatre boxes and at a White House reception and at a fencing match, and their broughams and motors from the windows of Mrs. Randolph's School, she was not sure she could be right in suspecting that a woman's charms and her taste in hats sometimes survive intelligence and even education. She also looked out of Mrs. Randolph's windows at the notable funerals and the other triumphs which enliven the avenues of Washington, and she observed the younger members of the diplomatic corps in uniforms which reminded her of George the Fourth, King of England, and of Lohengrin, son of Parsifal. Conversation with them seemed to be still more unlikely than conversation with the wives of their chiefs, and since her confidence in the printed page had not been killed by the Prophet Isaiah, she turned to the novels of the authorities who signed themselves Ouida and The Duchess. She had no reason to doubt their accuracy when they reported the private conversation of attachés and guardsmen, or to doubt their accuracy when they described the emotion called love, and she found them much more satisfactory than she had found the Prophet Isaiah's descriptions of the emotion called religion. The affection which The Duchess's heroines felt for the tall young gentlemen who took them out of the schoolroom and seated them at the head of long dinner tables in large country houses, did not seem to be very different from the affection she had felt for Cary Fairfax, and although the affection Ouida's heroines felt for their tall young guardsmen seemed to be very different indeed, she was sure that Cigarette was not a model for a southern lady, and she had no doubt that she understood the exact nature of well-bred love. But the affection the tall young gentlemen felt for Molly Bawn and Phyllis and tender Dolores was evidently more ardent than the affection the little boy from the Sunday school had felt for her, and she closed a book called Beauty's Daughters with the decision that reading love stories would be too painful until she could read them and remember with pride the flaming but respectful language of her own first love-letter.

Katharine Faraday did not quite realize that Mrs. Randolph considered the government of the United States one of the departments of her school—a department as important as her department of English poetry, and almost as important of something which she called the history of art and which she taught in her own sitting-room, standing beside her own Carrara marble copy of the Cupid and Psyche who were modelled by a sculptor called Canova, and surrounded by her own hand-painted copies of the Sistine Madonna and the Holy Night and the Mater Dolorosa and the Last Communion of Saint Jerome. And since Katharine Faraday did not realize that Mrs. Randolph considered the capitol of the United States the laboratory of her department of politics and government, she did not understand why she and Margaret Cameron and Isabel Ambler were allowed to visit the halls of congress alone, and to look down from the members' gallery on the Honourable Leonidas Livingston and the Honourable Claude Kitchin and the Honourable Nicholas Longworth and the Honourable Joseph Cannon and the Honourable and heroic Richmond Pearson Hobson, and on a tall representative whose feet rested beside the banana peeling on his desk, and who was more concerned with the banana in his right hand than with the eloquence of the Honourable William Sulzer. And since she did not know that Mrs. Randolph considered the Library of Congress as much a part of her school's library as the two hundred calf-bound volumes she had brought from the banks of the Rapidan River to the long front room on her second floor, Katharine Faraday did not understand why she and Margaret Cameron were allowed to make their researches alone, when they could not sit alone in the National Theatre and see an actress called Viola Allen in a play called The White Sister. Katharine Faraday would have liked to make her researches alone occasionally, since they were sometimes made in a large and clearly illustrated book called Gray's Anatomy, which proved that George Faraday was made like other men, and sometimes in an unsatisfactory book called Sherard's Life of Oscar Wilde, and she did not like to share all her curiosity even with Margaret Cameron. When Mrs. Randolph found herself unable to allow one of her young ladies to walk down Pennsylvania Avenue alone, Katharine Faraday remembered that on the afternoons when she had walked down Courtland Street because she did not have on her best hat and her pride would not allow her to walk on Peachtree Street, she had never seen a nun come out of Saint Joseph's Infirmary without another nun walking virtuously beside her. But when she discovered that a girl in a green coat and skirt and a black velvet turban can sit beside a girl in a blue coat and skirt and a black velvet turban without discouraging the glances of two very young men in blue serge suits and grey felt hats, she decided that nuns are probably better chaperoned by their coifs and their habits and their crucifixes than they are by each other. She would have been a little mortified if the two young men had not given up their own researches just after she and Margaret Cameron gave up hope of discovering exactly why Oscar Wilde was sent to Reading Gaol, and if they had not found her pointing out

Melpomene's swirling scarlet robes to Margaret Cameron, and telling her that even as a child she had been able to prefer the drawings of an illustrator called Wenzell to the drawings of another illustrator called Gibson. When the two young men took off their grey felt hats, one of them assured Katharine Faraday and Margaret Cameron that his name was Leroy Williams and that he had been born in Mississippi, and the other one assured them that his name was Crozier McIntosh, and that he had been born in Tennessee, and Katharine Faraday could not bring herself to refuse her compatriots' invitation to have some tea at the New Willard Hotel. But when she was dropping a slice of lemon and a lump of sugar and six cloves and two candied cherries into her tea, she felt as publicly depraved as Hester Prynne standing on her scaffold and holding her baby against her scarlet letter. And when she was walking up Mrs. Randolph's well-scrubbed steps, she waved a polite hand towards the corner of Connecticut Avenue, but she told Margaret Cameron that apparently the lack of an introduction did not make men any more interesting.

Katharine Faraday's mother was convinced that Atlanta would be more likely to notice the transformation of her duckling if it did not see her again until her last grey feather was blanched and she had acquired the last curve of perfect cygneous grace. But since she saw no reason why Katharine Faraday's father and brothers should observe her transformation, and no probability that they would observe it, Katharine Faraday came down from Washington to enjoy her family's society at a little hotel in the mountains of North Carolina—a little hotel which happy memories of her children's happy summers had never allowed Katharine Faraday's mother to desert except during the years when the interests of Marian and Eleanor Faraday had persuaded her that she could not resist revisiting the scenes of her own triumphs at the Greenbrier White Sulphur Springs. Katharine Faraday's father sat on the porch of his little cottage, and smoked better cigars than he could afford to smoke, and discussed the possibility that the next administration would be a Democratic administration and the probability that the hams cured in the state of Georgia would shortly equal the hams cured in the state of Virginia. Her mother sat on the farther end of the porch, and conversed with those ladies whose name and towns she found sufficiently distinguished to be remembered, and whenever a gentleman approached her end of the porch, she dropped her husband's largest handkerchief over the incredibly small and incredibly perfect tucks with which she was adorning the first frock that would be worn by her first grandchild. Alex Faraday enjoyed his second vacation from the University of Georgia in the society of a girl whose skirts were tied tightly around her nicely diminished ankles, and whose light brown hair was augmented by rows of neatly rolled puffs and by bands of light blue satin ribbon. Alex Faraday had not yet arrived at an age when he could walk with a sister through the fields where he had helped her to fill tin buckets with blackberries or through the wood where he had helped her to dig strips of moss so green and so thick and so long that they could carpet the rooms which can be economically arranged between the roots of old oak-trees, and Katharine Faraday did not spend quite one morning in lonely visits to the wood where she had dug poison ivy along with her moss. She did not know that she disliked being alone because she liked conversation more than any other human diversion, or that her natural fondness for conversation had increased since horror of becoming the author of an American novel had made it her only opportunity of convincing her acquaintances that she was uncommonly clever and uncommonly erudite for a girl who was not quite eighteen years old. But she was destined to live and to die without ever suggesting that she would enjoy the conversation of any human being who had not suggested that he would enjoy conversation with her, and she hung a yellow hammock between two oak-trees which were easily visible from the porch of the little hotel, and then she laid herself carefully down in the hammock and began to read the third volume of the history of England which was written by the first Lord Macaulay. She was not much interested in knowing that every window from Whitehall to Piccadilly was lighted up in honor of King William and Queen Mary, and since she had noticed that Lord Macaulay's style was very unlike Mr. Beerbohm's, she was not surprised when she discovered that he had not enjoyed the advantage of an Oxford education. But she did not suspect her father of being wrong in believing that Lord Macaulay's style was delightful to every one except herself—not any more than she suspected him of being wrong in believing Jesus died so that she might have eternal life, and not any more than she suspected her mother of being wrong in believing that blue frocks always make the most satisfactory approach to a face the colour of a freesia, and that yellow and red frocks always make the most satisfactory approach to black hair. And since she did not often doubt that a fortunately timed spraining of an ankle would shortly introduce her to her destined husband, or that her destined husband was a tall young Englishman who sprang from a family at least as ancient as the Howards or the Percys, and who would shortly become a prime minister as young as the youngest prime minister in the novels of Benjamin Disraeli, she was sure that a knowledge of English history would be more useful at her dinners than it would have been at the tables to which Phyllis and tender Dolores were triumphantly led in black velvet from Worth. Neither was there any discussion of King William in the novel called The Rosary, but it sent her to bed early every evening so that she could plan carefully punctuated little stories about Katharine Faraday and a husband as handsome and as romantically blinded as young Mr. Dalmain, or about Katharine Faraday and a husband as handsome and as romantically broken in the hunting field as the young Mr. Dugdale to whom The Duchess had married the younger heroine of Beauty's Daughters. Her destined husband looked very much like a young actor called Donald Brian, whom Katharine Faraday had seen dancing among dozens of tall and lovely show girls who were dressed in all the shades of violet and lilac and lavender and orchid which her mother denied to all brunettes. And he always wore a perfect top-hat and a perfect morning coat when he accompanied her to the garden-party at which her plumed hat from Virot and her lace frock from Paquin, and her lace parasol from a shop not yet selected, and her audacious cleverness, excited the admiration of the King of England. Until the British embassy had gone into mourning on the sixth of May, she had thought that the presentation would be still more interesting to her and to King Edward the Seventh if the tall young husband had become a beautiful memory a correct two years before the garden party, but the photographs of King George the Fifth did not encourage the idea of becoming the first royal favorite since Diane de Poitiers who understood that perpetual black and white can always delicately suggest a perpetual rival in heaven.

Katharine Faraday sat on the little hotel's porch long enough to hear Robert Carter respectfully spoken of as a Virginian gentleman who differed from other Virginian gentlemen in cultivating a taste for learning which twenty thousand dollars a year and his name made unnecessary, and she was pleased when the third volume of Lord Macaulay's history drew him to her yellow hammock. She did not suppose that he could be her destined husband, since he was an American, and since he already had a wife who wore limp white silk gowns. But she thought that conversation with him would be good practice for the conversations she might some day have with the brilliant young peers for whom she would pour out tea with milk and three lumps of sugar, and which might equal anything in the novels of Benjamin Disraeli. Her mother had told her that a woman must always persuade a man to talk about the subject he is interested in, and since her mother had never suspected that Katharine Faraday might ever be interested in any subject a man could be interested in, she had told her that a woman must always expect to be bored. Her mother had also told her that no southern lady had ever sat in a hammock with any man, and Katharine Faraday sat down on the more uncomfortable end of a bench before she asked Robert Carter to tell her just how the pyramids of Egypt were built. She did not know that there are more than three pyramids in Egypt or that Robert Carter was beginning a story which would necessarily be a serial story, but she did not have to act an interest in a learned narrative which was addressed exclusively to her. He did not neglect a dynasty, and before he had reached a millennium which had no idea that it was the fourth millennium before Christ, his silk clad wife had begun to find the altitude bad for her blood pressure. Katharine Faraday's mother lived in a world where gentlemen did not return from the bourne of marriage any oftener than they returned from the bourne of death, and she decided that her youngest daughter must take advantage of an opportunity to read Robert

Browning's poems with a scholarly lady who lived only two miles away. Robert Carter went to Cape May with his wife, and Katharine Faraday hung her yellow hammock between two locust-trees which were not visible from the porch of the little hotel. Sometimes she read Lord Macaulay's history, even though she had begun to doubt that her husband would be a tall young Englishman, and sometimes she read a book called Below the Cataracts. Sometimes she laid her left cheek against the consolingly inscribed fly-leaf of the book called Below the Cataracts and planned carefully punctuated little stories about the evening, a correct year away, when Robert Carter would return to her one week after his tailor had removed the black bands from the sleeves of his coats. And sometimes she did not read anything or plan anything, and a fountain rose and fell and dropped its electric spray through her thin brown body.

When Katharine Faraday went back to Mrs. Randolph's school and to the observation of ladies who had achieved birth in Europe and marriage with ambassadors, she had finished reading Below the Cataracts, and the fountain did not very often drop its electric spray underneath the delicate brown line which ran down what she still called her stomach. She had begun to fear that the story of Katharine Faraday and Robert Carter would not end as happily as the story of Molly Bawn or the story of Phyllis, and that Katharine Faraday was the heroine of a story as sad as the story of the little mermaid and the prince with golden hair. When Isabel Ambler told the story of the very handsome and very brilliant and very aristocratic young gentleman to whom she would certainly have been already engaged if he had not died of typhoid fever in August, Katharine Faraday could not tell her the story of Katharine Faraday and Robert Carter, since she could not say she had wanted something which fate apparently did not intend to give her. But she restrained a noticeable number of tears when she sat in the twilight and joined Isabel Ambler and Margaret Cameron in the melancholy songs they sang between oranges and chocolates, and Isabel Ambler became the third of the intimate friends who were entirely satisfactory to Katharine Faraday's mother. Katharine Faraday enjoyed the society of an intimate friend who was also acquainted with grief, and she knew just how many of the young gentlemen who came to Mrs. Randolph's dances agreed with her own verdict that Isabel Ambler was the only one of Mrs. Randolph's young ladies who was prettier than Katharine Faraday, and just how often her mother had told her that a girl should never choose her intimate friends among girls who are likely to be overlooked by men. But even without her mother's advice, her conscience did not hurt her when the necessity of protecting her own masculine interests forced her to tell Isabel Ambler that she was prettier when her red hair was straight than when it was waved. It did not hurt her even when those interests forced her to say that although blue was not usually becoming to girls with red hair, forget-me-not blue was so becoming to Isabel Ambler that she must consent to borrow Katharine Faraday's embroidered chiffon tunic. When Isabel Ambler made the mistake of accepting her opinion and her blue tunic, Katharine Faraday did not think she showed an understanding of human nature which might have been expected of a girl whose forefathers had understood their fellow men well enought to govern the commonwealth of Virginia. And when Isabel Ambler could not bring herself to join Katharine Faraday and Margaret Cameron in fitting together their bits of information about bridal nights, and about their connection with the subsequent birth of a baby, Katharine Faraday almost decided to go down to Wilmington and see a mere North Carolina Christmas in Margaret Cameron's more inquiring company. But she was almost sure that her fountain would begin to rise and fall again when she crossed the Potomac into Robert Carter's native commonwealth—even though he had doubtless gone back to the banks of the River Nile—and she was sure that after she had seen the white doorway of the house in which he was born, she would lie down with her left cheek against the inscribed fly-leaf of Below the Cataracts, and that she would go to sleep feeling its radiant spray again. She also thought that if Virginia had been able to create Robert Carter and Isabel Ambler's lost Harrison, some other brilliant and aristocratic young men must still survive there. And since she could not read Florence Barclay's new novel, or even go on with another story of young love called The Ordeal of Richard Feverel, she did not want to wait any longer for her first flaming but respectful love-letter. She was sure the young man she would charm in Richmond was not her destined husband, and she did not consider the quality of his forefathers or the quality of his letters. She did not think of him at all when she first saw him, since she had just walked slowly past the house where Robert Carter had been born forty years before. But he did not know that she was tingling with radiance because she was remembering a thin sun-burned face, and he did not wait until she had gone back to Washington before he made her a declaration as flaming and as respectful as any declaration Molly Bawn or Lucy Feverel ever heard. When she looked at the first man who had ever grown damp around the eyes when he looked at her, she ran up the mahogany railed stairs. And when Isabel Ambler's mother told her that his great-grandfather was not a man whom his descendants would have invited to dinner, she remembered her fear that she was one of those girls who appeal to the wrong kind of man. But on the first morning after she was back in Washington, the postman's ring at the door left her unable to hear Mrs. Randolph's reading of the Protestant Episcopal Church's Order for Morning Prayer. And when she opened the first letter which had ever been written to her on the large black-printed sheets of a large corporation, she read with complete satisfaction his description of his uncomfortable emotions when she ran up Mrs. Ambler's stairs and the curtain of his life went down on an empty stage. She put the letter between the last two distressing pages of the story of Richard and Lucy Feverel, and between the distressing chapters she read it as contentedly as she had read Louisa Alcott's description of a Thanksgiving dinner at Plumfield between the turkey and the mince pie of her own tenth Thanksgiving dinner.

Katharine Faraday's distaste for American literature was increased by Mrs. Randolph's belief that every young lady should read a novel called The House of Seven Gables and a narrative poem called Giles Corey, but her information was increased. And since she was sure that Mrs. Robert Carter's blood pressure was not dangerously high, she melted a candle she thought was wax and she modelled a little doll and painted very blue veins on it. She dressed her doll in comparatively limp white silk and tied a black taffeta ribbon around its listless hair, and then she stuck seven long black English pins into its blue veins. She had no more confidence in the efficacy of black pins than she had in the efficacy of prayer, but twice every month she carefully read the announcements of elegant deaths in a paper called Vogue, and once every month she read them in a paper called Town and Country, since she was sure Mrs. Robert Carter's last words would be a request that her death should be announced to her world in those two periodicals. She always wondered if the important ladies who died in Chicago and San Francisco and New Orleans had benefited the world and their successors as much as Mrs. Carter's death would, but she was sure that if the pins did not raise Mrs. Carter's blood pressure to a fatal two hundred and fifty during the decorous season of Lent, she would not inconvenience her sisters by dying incongruously just after Easter, and when Palm Sunday came without the announcement that the world had lost another Carter, she decided that the story of Katharine Faraday and Robert Carter was complete. She found that she did not enjoy improving the heroine's conversation in a story which was finished, and that she could not go back to the literary and theatrical heroes whom she had found satisfactory before the tenth of July. And she found that she did not enjoy discussing the details of bridal nights with Margaret Cameron, since she could not discuss them without remembering that Mr. and Mrs. Robert Carter were probably engaged in another such night at that exact moment, even allowing for the difference of time between the District of Columbia and the banks of the Nile. Even Nathaniel Hawthorne was obliged to admit that men and women are sometimes happily married, and since she did not want to read Treasure Island again, she began to read a book called The Origin of Species. But the satisfaction of being found with such a celebrated book on her knees did not compensate her for reading about so much mating and so much reproduction, and she lived through a week when she could not read anything except a geometry, and when a hot bath at night was no greater luxury than a cool bath in the morning, and when a first hour in bed was as desolate as it would have been with iced water in her hot water-bag.

On the eighth of April, Katharine Faraday was unable to eat any Smithfield ham because she had decided that the story of Katharine Faraday and Robert Carter was complete, and on the twelfth of April, she was unable to eat any shrimp salad, or even to drink a cup of chocolate, after she had read her name on the same envelope with the West Point postmark. She had no hope that she would ever feel the passion of love again, but she knew that every young lady should dance either at West Point or at Annapolis before her nineteenth birthday. And since she knew that very few young ladies succeed in being married without ever having been to a dance, she was willing to go to a dance at which a card entirely filled with adequate names would be waiting to save her from agonies of suspense. Mrs. Randolph regretted that Cadet Lewis Gordon should have a roommate who had been born so far north as the state of Minnesota, but she saw no impropriety in his request that Mildred Cobb would satisfy the curiosity of his roommate by bringing Katharine Faraday up to West Point with her. Neither did she see any impropriety in Cadet James Fuller's letter to Katharine Faraday, which she found sufficiently grammatical and sufficiently respectful to confirm her hope that even since the Spanish War there were gentlemen in the American army, and to confirm Katharine Faraday's hope that there would not be many young men of the wrong kind. On the evening of the twelfth of April, Katharine Faraday laid herself down in a bath of very hot water exactly one hygienic hour after she had swallowed her fourth spoonful of charlotte russe, and then she read James Fuller's letter over nine times. At half past nine o'clock, she slipped into bed, and she lay down with the backs of her hands pressed flat against her legs and her feet pressed flat against a very hot water-bag, and then she composed the first episode of the story of Katharine Faraday and James Fuller. On the afternoon of the thirteenth of April, she walked down to the public library with the youngest of Mrs. Randolph's reduced gentlewomen, and since she thought that all librarians are eternally virgin priestesses in the temple of knowledge, she looked with curiosity and respect and condescension at the girl in the white blouse and the blue skirt who stamped the date in the back of a book called Life at West Point and a book called A History of Minnesota and a book called The Music Dramas of Richard Wagner. On the evening of the thirteenth of April, she read about the required method of bed-making in cadets' quarters and about classes in fencing and riding and tactics and about summer camp, and then she read about Indians and flour and the source of the Mississippi River, and about a governor called John Johnson, until she was sure that she could talk to James Fuller about the things in which she supposed he must be interested. On the afternoon of the fourteenth of April, she read about the music drama called Parsifal, and she played the motif of the grail and the motif of faith and the motif of the lance so often that she was sure she would be more erudite than Mildred Cobb when they went to the Metropolitan Opera House on Friday afternoon. Then she ran narrow blue satin ribbon around the neck of her best white linen lawn combination, and slightly wider blue satin ribbon around its waist, and she carefully whipped on the Valenciennes lace she had been meaning to mend ever since the combination came up from the laundry after Mrs. Randolph's Valentine dance. And then she packed the new blue foulard her mother had sent her the week before, and her white serge coat and skirt and the white lace blouse she wore with them, and her lemon yellow chiffon cloth evening gown, and Margaret Cameron's white satin petticoat embroidered with roses, and Isabel Ambler's leghorn hat with the blue willow plume and her gold slippers and stockings. She put on a blue crêpe de chine blouse with a wide scalloped frill which was intended to veil the flatness of her chest, and a narrow blue basket cloth skirt which mounted four fashionable inches above her waist, and a short blue basket cloth coat with sleeves which ended three fashionable inches below her sharp elbows, and a wide blue straw hat with six full-blown Killarney roses around its crown, and a pair of black patent leather pumps, and a pair of sixteen button black glacé gloves.

Isabel Ambler and Margaret Cameron and Mrs. Randolph's youngest gentlewoman went to the New York train with her, and she lay down in her berth and stretched her hands flat against her legs, and then she began to compose a more romantic and more carefully punctuated episode in the story of Katharine Faraday and James Fuller. She knew that unless she sprained an ankle in Rock Creek Park within the next six weeks, and unless a tall young Englishman rode by on his devoted horse very soon after she had sprained her ankle, she would not be likely to find an English husband, since tall young English diplomats do not often ride down the streets of Atlanta, or even along the roads in the mountains of North Carolina. And she thought that if the next administration should be a Democratic administration, her father's influence might possibly help to make his son-in-law military attaché to the American embassy in London, and that she would then certainly be presented to King George the Fifth in the gardens of Buckingham Palace, and possibly to a young Irish duke who would implore her to fly with him to his castle beside the lakes of Killarney.

She knew that American army officers are sometimes wounded at target practice, and that Lieutenant James Fuller might easily be as romantically blinded as Garth Dalmain. But before Lieutenant James Fuller had been carried to the Walter Reed Hospital, and even before his devoted young wife had burned all the young Irish duke's flaming but respectful letters, and before she had knelt beside her husband's bed and kissed the bandage over each of his wounded eyes, Katharine Faraday was dreaming that she had walked up the branching stairs of Cullum Hall in her lemon yellow frock and Isabel Ambler's gold slippers, and that James Fuller was not in the ball-room or on the white balcony which looked down on the Hudson River. She woke up just as she was slipping between the unconcerned dancers, behind the little page who was dressed very much like the pages in the New Willard Hotel, and who was calling her to the telephone where she would surely hear James Fuller's voice.

Just before one o'clock on the afternoon of Good Friday, Katharine Faraday walked up the stairs of the Metropolitan Opera House and sat down in the broad scarlet seat beside Mildred Cobb's broad scarlet seat. Mildred Cobb had been living on West Eighty-Fifth Street for nearly a year, but Katharine Faraday was sure that her wide blue hat would stand a comparison with Mildred Cobb's wide black hat, and when she looked down at the curving line of boxes, she decided that it would stand a comparison with the hats of the great ladies whom she had read about in the corinthian prose of a writer called Cholly Knickerbocker. She felt that she was about to take an examination in the motifs of Parsifal, and since Mildred Cobb had gone over to the Church of England so recently that she spoke of Good Friday as if it celebrated the heroism of one of her own eminent ancestors, Katharine Faraday was as concerned about passing the examination with distinction as she was about her hat. When thirty-two violins had played the motif of the Eucharist, to which Mildred Cobb listened with the devotion proper to a member of an apostolic church sitting beside a member of John Calvin's church, and when two harps had joined them in repeating it with admirably executed arpeggios, and when the violins had slipped down to play it again in the correctly relative minor, Katharine Faraday was relieved to discover that Richard Wagner had no idea of allowing his audiences to miss any of the motifs he had taken the trouble to invent, or even the motifs he had only taken the trouble to borrow. She settled down to meditate on Mildred Cobb's description of James Fuller's black hair and grey eyes and long legs, and of the very masculine darkness of his upper lip in spite of shaves twice as frequent as the regulations of the United States Military Academy required. Katharine Faraday had not yet heard that a man who is fond of his mother is the victim of a disease called an Oedipus complex, and when a robust soprano called Olive Fremstad put on the seductive garments of Kundry and lay down among the large and brilliant cotton flowers to ensnare young Parsifal by singing about his happy infancy, she came up above the music long enough to decide that the ladies of the diplomatic corps were better models for rousing passions which were honourable as well as ardent. But before virtuous innocence had triumphed over Kundry's prophetic knowledge of Freudian psychology, she had slipped down through the waves of the music to rest on the shifting sand of her own ideas and her own emotions, and her own fears that she might have to go back to Mrs. Randolph's School and admit that she had not been asked to come up to West Point again. When the curtains closed on the last bowing line, she was still wondering why men can ask girls to dance with them and and to marry them, and if it is because girls can have babies and men cannot.

If Katharine Faraday had not brought herself up on the literature of the Beardsley period, she would certainly not have developed an early taste for epigrams, and for the constant repetition of her belief that nothing is so immodest as modesty. But The Dolly Dialogues and The Importance of Being Earnest were not responsible for the annoyance she always felt when she spent a night with a modest girl whose mother had produced more children than her father had produced bathrooms, and who felt obliged to slip her nightgown over her head as she slipped her frock off her feet, and then to fumble tediously with the ribbons and the buttons of her camisole and her combination, and with the strings and the hooks of her corset. For five years, Katharine Faraday had supposed that Mildred Cobb used a nainsook nightgown as a screen because she had long heavy breasts weighted down by unused milk, and she still supposed there was some connection between their heaviness and the fondness for robust stories which Katharine Faraday's mammy also remembered in two generations of that family. But ten minutes after she had begun turning away from Mrs. Rutherford Cobb's suffering between the impropriety of being seen with her collar unhooked and the impropriety of letting either her own daughter or Mrs. Alexander Faraday's daughter spend an unchaperoned minute in a hotel set in such masculine surroundings as the reservation of the United States Military Academy, she realized that Mildred Cobb's modesty was not inherited from the ladies who sent her into brassieres at the age of twelve, and she began to disobey her mother and to believe that Mrs. Rutherford Cobb would not feel obliged to be so ladylike unless her mammy had really seen Mrs. Rutherford Cobb's mother walking barefoot in a cotton field. Before she opened the calf-skin bag which Eleanor Faraday had found unworthy to hold the white crêpe de chine nightgown she was sure a southern lady should not have worn even on her bridal night, Katharine Faraday sat down on the farthest of the three white iron beds with her back towards her most intimate friend and her most intimate friend's mother. She pulled on the black silk stockings whose clocks she admired so much that she had saved them since Christmas for her possible reunion with Robert Carter, and then she slipped off her nainsook combination and wished she could walk over to the mirror and be sure that she looked like the Degas drawing she had seen the day before. Then she powdered her thin brown body so ceremonially that she remembered the lustral rites with which Aphrodite had prepared her soft pink body for the visits of Ares—since the afternoon when Robert Carter had sat on the more comfortable end of a bench and described the oldest Trojan city for her, Katharine Faraday had never made the vulgar mistake of calling authentically Greek gods by merely Roman names—and she slipped on her linen lawn combination and tied its narrow blue ribbons over her flat chest and its slightly wider blue ribbons over the delicate brown line which still ran down what she still called her stomach. When she had hooked her Alice blue foulard down her left shoulder and around her left arm, and when Mrs. Rutherford Cobb had succeeded in hooking Mildred Cobb's green foulard around Mildred Cobb's painful corset and Mildred Cobb had succeeded in pinning her mother's veil in a line worthy of a crape toque from Crocker, Katharine Faraday felt that she could go back to the same side of the room with her most intimate friend and her most intimate friend's mother, and that she could stand in front of the mirror long enough to pin on Isabel Ambler's leghorn hat with the blue willow plume. Though she was not sure the Italian ambassadress had been sitting among the ladies of the diplomatic corps whom she had conscientiously observed during the afternoon when four young midshipmen touched the scarlet satin hearts on the tight fencing jackets of four young attachés who had dined out too often, and even though she was never sure Naples or Cincinnati had not provided the ambassador with a wife, she had not opened a hat-box since that afternoon without telling a new audience that she could not hope to settle a hat as elegantly aslant as a lady who had enjoyed the advantage of growing up in the presence of the leaning tower of Pisa. Instead of smiling the brave and melancholy smile which even the most conservative fashion-plates were allowing to faces framed in the best crape, Mrs. Rutherford Cobb continued to look and to speak as if her daughter and her daughter's most intimate friend were somehow slightly responsible for Judge Rutherford Cobb's taking off. But Katharine Faraday began becoming reconciled to the presence of Judge Rutherford Cobb's relict when she found herself arranging the phrases in which she would risk being struck by lightning or leprosy long enough to compare the number of Mrs. Rutherford Cobb's weepings with the number of Jesus Christ's weepings as they were chronicled by Luke and John, and the complete absence of Mrs. Rutherford Cobb's smile with the complete absence of Jesus Christ's smiles as they were chronicled by the minister's daughter. She became entirely reconciled to Mrs. Rutherford Cobb when the comparison had acquired a finish which kept it in her repertoire long after she had learned that allusions to the leaning tower of Pisa were hardly evidence of erudition, and until she had ceased to feel that a sufficiently casual mention of Jesus Christ redeemed a dull sentence as certainly as a strip of pimento redeemed three pale stalks of asparagus. But Mrs. Rutherford Cobb handed her Cadet James Fuller's correctly engraved card before the comparison was arranged in the finished form which completed Margaret Cameron's conversion to the belief that very few emotions are pleasanter than the emotion of being shocked. Katharine Faraday thought that the name on the card made her feel just as she had always felt when she was turning her mother's doorknob on Christmas morning and just as she had always felt when the footlights flashed on the beautiful face of Queen Elizabeth and the handsome face of William Shakespeare which adorned the curtain of the Grand Opera House on Peachtree Street, but she laid the card inside the second best handkerchief in her little blue leather bag, and she continued to find the Italian ambassadress's slant inimitable until Mrs. Rutherford Cobb had preceded her daughter so far down the West Point Hotel's straight steep stairway that she was unlikely to risk her exhausted heart by coming back up to her mirror and having her veil pinned even more smoothly.

Then Katharine Faraday opened her little blue bag again, and she began the cosmetic anthology she had collected while she was discovering that ambassadresses and princesses and countesses and mere baronesses are painted to look painted instead of being painted to look pretty, and which she had translated and abridged for the purpose of rivalling the prettiest of Mrs. Randolph's young ladies. When she thought that Cadet James Fuller had expected her as long as the anthology would justify, and when she had dropped her tan coat because she did not like it well enough to feel cold, Katharine Faraday walked down the steep stairs and into the drawing-room which was filled with cadets and with the young ladies of all the more fashionable schools and with chaperones and with a very large rubber-tree. She did not wait to compare Cadet James Fuller's black hair and grey eyes with the brown hair and the brown eyes of Cadet Lewis Gordon or with the eyes of Cadet Pringle Rhett, which were as much fairer than his face as his name and the memory of Sarah Rutledge had led her to expect, or with any of the eyes or any of the hair she could see between the branches of the rubber-tree. She did not wait to dance with any of the five hundred and forty-nine fellow cadets to whom the regulations of the United States Military Academy entitled Cadet James Fuller, or to hear their conversation. When she walked past the lofty victory which her researches told her was a commemoration of one hundred and eighty-eight officers and two thousand and forty-two soldiers of the Regular Army who were killed in battle, or who died of wounds in the Civil War, but which Cadet James Fuller told her was the Monument to Southern Marksmanship, Katharine Faraday was sure the wrong kind of young man could not possibly be so tactful, and she was almost sure the curtain had gone up on a first act which would be worthy of its scenery.

The romantic tragedy of Katharine Faraday and James Fuller differed from most other dramas in raising its curtain directly on the first meeting of its heroine and its hero, and in never allowing the heroine to deprive the dialogue of her clever lines by walking off into silencing and concealing wings. But Katharine Faraday did not enjoy the second scene of its first act. Even with a path called Flirtation Walk for a back-drop, she could not forget that the correct fifty feet of the Hudson River might not be the back-drop of the act's last scene, or that the hero's last lines might not be a repetition of his earnest request that Katharine Faraday would come back to West Point on the first possible Saturday afternoon, or that his last lines might not be half drowned by the impatient West Shore train to which the heroine's frightened protest against risking his liberty had not prevented his accompanying her. When Cadet Pringle Rhett occupied the pause between his two dances with the formality of his request that she would allow him to make out her hop-card for the first Saturday in May, she provided for her victory in the eyes of Isabel Ambler and Margaret Cameron by telling him that she would not be able to believe he really wanted her unless he wrote to her and asked her to come back, and she was comforted by the realization that they could not possibly guess how much lighter his eyes were than the face which framed them as dull oak ledges framed the pale hot water of the primeval bathtubs in which she had passed so much of her earlier youth. She remembered the ardent little boy at the First Presbyterian Sunday School and the calm little boy at the Calhoun Street School, and when she began her last waltz with Cadet James Fuller she was wondering if men she did not like would always be the only men who could discover the charms which she was sure she had, but which she was not at all sure of the world's ability to appreciate. She was also thinking that any bar of the orchestra's deliberately depressing hesitation between Home Sweet Home and Army Blue would provide a sufficiently appropriate accompaniment for James Fuller's interrogative hope that this would not be their last dance together. And when she looked out into the hall at the officer of the day and his apparently infallible watch and his expectant drummer, she was sure she was much unhappier than Floria Tosca would have been if she had known there were six bullets in the six muskets which would be aimed at the heart of Mario Cavaradossi when the Holy Father's officer of the day lowered his sword. When James Fuller spoke his interrogative hope as Katharine Faraday walked back across the parade ground with him, she wondered if he thought stars a more appropriate accompaniment than an orchestra, or if he had heard a favourable verdict from his fellow cadets while he was presumably finding his cap and she was presumably finding her coat. But the possibility that he might modestly doubt the perfection of his own taste in girls was not the reason why she told him that she would not be able to believe he really wanted her unless he wrote to her and asked her to come back. And it did not keep her from enjoying even the modesty of the slow undressing two comparatively unaccepted invitations allowed her, or from putting up with the story of Mildred Cobb's superior triumphs and the story of the sufferings Mrs. Rutherford Cobb had endured for the sake of her daughter and for the sake of Mrs. Alexander Faraday's daughter. But it was one of the reasons why she lay down on her face with the backs of her hands pressed flat against the West Point Hotel's sheets and the palms of her hands pressed flat against her legs, and why she felt the electric spray fall down her arms while she let her mind nestle against the suspicion that she wanted to come back to West Point because she wanted to see James Fuller's black hair and his grey eyes and his broad shoulders and his long legs, and why she did not mind knowing that this would be the only night when she would be happy until the night when she could lie down beside a pillow under which James Fuller's politely personal second note lay on his politely impersonal first note.

During the first hour of five nights, Katharine Faraday tried not to touch the tender blue spot which she was sure one of the round brass buttons on James Fuller's dress uniform had left on her freesia chest, and she tried to think of everything except that she was only less unhappy than she would have been if she had been justly accused of murder, and if a jury had deliberated her fate for a hundred and twenty hours. During the next eight hours of five nights, she dreamed that she was just taking James Fuller's letter from a postman. And during the fifteen hours of five days, she longed to draw the shelter of a sheet between her unforgotten suspense and a world which might enjoy knowing that she wanted something fate might not intend to give her. When she saw her name on the same envelope with the West Point postmark, and then saw that it had been written there by Pringle Rhett, she was only less unable to read his letter than she would have been to read a slip of paper which recorded that she had been found guilty of murder with a recommendation to the mercy of the court, and for half a day she could not give Isabel Ambler and Margaret Cameron an opportunity of pretending to be glad that the right kind of young man had asked Katharine Faraday to dance a second evening at West Point. But when she saw her name on another envelope with the West Point postmark, and then saw James Fuller's name on the fourth satisfactory page of a sheet of paper distinguished by the crest of the class of nineteen hundred and twelve, she saw the black postmark printed in scarlet and alabaster and sapphire, and shining below forty-eight golden stars and set above the shining notes of The Star-Spangled Banner. The radiant spray shot up from under her delicate brown line to her throat, and the letter from her mother, which discussed only the number of George and Arthur Faraday's clients and the beauties of Marian Faraday's daughter, was apparently composed of words as red and as white and as blue as the words in which Sarah Rutledge announced that only six months would pass before Katharine Faraday could have the honour of preceding her to the altar of Saint Michael's Church.

Until George Faraday came up to Washington and took Katharine Faraday to dinner at the New Willard Hotel, he had never been even a minor character in her own story of her own life except on the Christmas morning when he had fainted in a relaxed garment and left her as unwilling to become a man as she was to become a woman. She remembered that his authoritative knock had often obliged her to jump out of agreeably hot water while she was reading a brilliant dialogue between Dolly, Countess of Mickleham and her Mr. Carter, and she remembered that at least three times a week his admiring family's dinner had been cut short by the disappearance of the only white vest in which he could possibly dine in Ansley Park or dance at the Piedmont Driving Club. She also remembered that she had enjoyed the inheritance of the hanging walnut shelves he had filled with the tales of a patriotic Englishman called G. A. Henty and with large flat periodicals called The Golden

Days. But she had not begun to suspect that The Cat of Bubastes and The Young Carthaginian and In Greek Waters had a certain responsibility for the Mediterranean tastes which led Robert Carter to describe the science of pyramid building for her, or that the disappearance of the white vests had a certain responsibility for making her the only member of her family who could not take the serious view of the Piedmont Driving Club which might have made her a less unsatisfactory partner for its members, or that his first six glasses of champagne had a certain responsibility for her unfortunate habit of thinking about the afternoons when her tall young husband would take her out to garden parties instead of thinking about the nights when he would probably enjoy lying by her side. When she sat across a little table from George Faraday and drank three sips of water and discussed her most fashionable subjects while he drank two large cocktails, she was not surprised that he did not even offer her one of his cherries, and she did not suspect either the social or the biological soundness of his demonstration that southern gentlemen consider alcoholic beverages unsuited to the fragile organisms which are capable of nothing more energetic than producing twelve babies. But when he proved the veracity of the New Willard Hotel's cocktails by giving her a twenty-dollar bill and a ten-dollar bill so golden that he might have received them directly from the Bureau of Printing and Engraving, she was sure she did not know him well enough to be sure he was too southern a gentleman to regret the temporary numbness of the two bumps of caution she had learned about at the Calhoun Street School. She declined a play whose program would have made a respectable addition to her big book, and she quivered off to sleep with her left hand pressed against the envelope in which the golden twenty-dollar bill and the golden ten-dollar bill were lying inside James Fuller's second note, and with her right hand pressed against the blue spot she was trying to keep blue and tender until she danced her second evening at West Point.

Katharine Faraday had never suffered the indignity of seeing the inside of an official prison, and her extreme distaste for experiencing the emotion called pity had never allowed her to visit a literary prison by reading more than one chapter of a novel called Little Dorrit or more than two stanzas of a poem called The Ballad of Reading Gaol. And until the necessity of receiving a love letter took her to stay with Isabel Ambler, she had never spent two consecutive nights with any one except her less satisfactorily married sister and the paternal aunt who was such a satisfactory Presbyterian that she was not much more satisfactory as an example of a hostess than she was an example of a Christian. Nevertheless, when her audience did not contain a girl who might just possibly become an intimate friend and whom she might just possibly like to visit, Katharine Faraday was fond of saying that if a month in jail did not usually leave a social stain as indelible as the ink with which her mother had insisted on marking all her washable garments, she would much rather pass a month as a prisoner than as a guest. She did not know she disliked being a guest because the number of people who could publicly neglect her, and who could see her publicly neglected, was necessarily exactly as large as the number of people with whom she could talk, but she was not exaggerating her convictions any more than experience had shown her she must exaggerate them if she expected to conquer in the competition of general conversation. She was certainly not exaggerating her distaste for Mrs. Rutherford Cobb's modesty or for Mrs. Rutherford Cobb's grief when James Fuller's third note and the assurance of not having to see them again allowed her to risk telling Isabel Ambler and Margaret Cameron that she was in love for the first time in her life—so much in love that, since the regulations of the United States Military Academy did not allow James Fuller to leave West Point, and since neither her brother's generosity nor her mother's ideas of propriety would allow her to buy the lonely freedom of a hotel, she was going to West Point with Mrs. Rutherford Cobb and Mildred Cobb on the very next Saturday, that she was then going down to be modest at Mrs. Rutherford Cobb's house on West Eighty-fifth Street for twelve days, and that she was going back to dance at West Point again in honour of the departing class of nineteen hundred and eleven. Her confidences were rewarded by Margaret Cameron's insistence that James Fuller must see Katharine Faraday in the red coat and the large hat made entirely of red silk poppy petals in which Midshipman De Roulhac Holt had found Margaret Cameron irresistible, and by Isabel Ambler's insistence that James Fuller must see Katharine Faraday in the orange crêpe de chine evening gown shirred with gold threads which Isabel Ambler could not possibly wear on the hot nights that would be inevitable at the Finals of the University of Virginia. Katharine Faraday had not begun to doubt the corrcctness of her mother's belief that red and yellow frocks make a desirable approach to black hair and to a face the colour of a freesia, and when she conscientiously looked out of a train window at the celebrated Delaware River, she was thinking with pleasure of the new collection of hats and frocks and coats in which James Fuller would see her. She was also thinking with pleasure of the matinées and the ice-cream sodas she had sacrificed on the altar of love, and which had placed another slightly less golden ten-dollar bill in the chamois bag that was making her tender blue spot pleasantly painful. And she was remembering with even more pleasure that for another year James Fuller would be forbidden a wife by the inexorable regulations of the United States Military Academy, that her more satisfactory brother-in-law—who always spoke with the conscious infallibility of a man who knows that his mortal remains will be buried in a vault—was fond of saying that no gentleman would think of mentioning marriage to a young lady until he could ask her to marry him as soon as the invitations to their wedding could be properly engraved and addressed to the proper residences, and that, since James Fuller was certainly not the wrong kind of young man, she need not begin to wonder whether or not he would beg her to become his wife. But since she had known for eight years that no southern lady ever allows any man to touch so much as her pocket handkerchief until he has begged her to become his wife, and since she had known for three years that no gentleman ever thinks of kissing any one except a disreputable girl until he has asked her to marry him, she did not think of what she might feel if James Fuller's lips touched her lips, or of what she might feel if his cheek touched her cheek. When she walked down to the drawing room of the West Point Hotel and saw him standing beside the tall rubber-tree, she felt that their reunion was history's most astonishing miracle, but she did not think about the touch of his hand against her hand, and she looked as calm as the wine which had been water one minute before. When she walked with him in front of the panoramic back-drop of Flirtation Walk, she did not think about the occasional touch of his assisting hand, and she did not think of finding her gloves too warm so that his hand might touch her arm instead of her long white glove, and she did not think about what he might be feeling when she sat beside him on a rock which she observed only as a well-placed theatrical property. She listened with very visible attention to his prophecies concerning the diversions she could enjoy if she would stay on for summer camp, but even if she had not known the temporal limits of one twenty-dollar bill and two ten-dollar bills, she would not have felt able to bear the strain of watching James Fuller's increasing or decreasing interest for even one week. When she opened her hop-card, she noticed with pleasure that James Fuller had not given Pringle Rhett even one pair of dances, that he had kept exactly half of her dances for himself, and that he had adorned the card's cord with a round brass button which might easily be the same button that had pressed against her yellow frock in April, and which would also make an easily displayed trophy as a hatpin. She was too unhappy to compare her triumphs with Mildred Cobb's triumphs when she was back in a West Shore train, but she was able to eat a chicken sandwich and to drink a glass of lemonade in the Weehawken station, and in the ferry-house she was able to remember that Aaron Burr's daughter had married a Charlestonian of excellent family, and that when she went to Sarah Rutledge's wedding in October, she might easily have an occasion to mention that she had been in the town where Aaron Burr proved himself a better shot than Alexander Hamilton. Although she had read the complete works of a writer called Richard Harding Davis and a great many other novels concerned entirely with the most fashionable residents of New York, she had never realised that no well-bred young lady should consider liking any young man whom she met in West Eighty-fifth Street, but she did not enjoy trying to be visibly interested in the civilian conversation of the young men in black coats and white ties whom Mrs. Rutherford Cobb conscientiously invited to dine with Mrs. Alexander Faraday's daughter. She went to dinner on the roof of the Waldorf-Astoria Hotel with one of the young men, and she did not enjoy herself, and she went to supper at the Beaux Arts Café with a young man whose latest cynical lyric had been printed in a weekly paper called Life, and she enjoyed only the succeeding hour when she was arranging the phrases in which she would relate the experiences of that evening to James Fuller. She went to lunch with another young man at a restaurant called Mouquin's, and she suffered when she went with the same young man to see a celebrated comedian with a very white face and a very red nose, and when she sat and tingled with radiance because she was remembering James Fuller without speaking of him, she was a complete social success at a party another young man gave for her in a large room with a fireplace and an encircling balcony and a samovar in it. And then she became exhausted from the effort of not mentioning West Point to young men who were apparently interested in poems and golf-sticks and stocks, and who were certainly not interested in tactics and sharpshooters' medals and the adornment of hop-cards, and she decided to be ill until she could return to military conversation and grey coats. When she walked down the West Point Hotel's stairs again, and saw James Fuller standing beside the rubber-tree in the crowded drawing room, she felt again that their reunion was a miracle, but she looked as calm as the green laurel-tree which had been Daphne pursued by Apollo one minute before, and she took his hand as she might have taken the high-veined hand of

Mrs. Randolph's oldest gentlewoman. She sat beside him all the afternoon on one of the stones of Fort Putnam, and she danced half the evening with him, and she stood with him on a white balcony and looked down at the Hudson River, and when the orchestra began its final hesitation between Army Blue and Home Sweet Home, she realized the propriety of his gloomy reference to a bugle-call named Taps, and she was even unhappier than the occasion required. But when she walked back across the parade ground with him, her unhappiness did not touch the serene core of her certainty that the publicly visible proofs of James Fuller's respectful and possibly ardent interest in Katharine Faraday would last twelve more hours, and that she would be able to lay her cheek against the photograph which had been made by a sufficiently well-known photographer, and to quiver with romance all the way from West Point to New York, all the way from New York to the little hotel in the mountains of North Carolina, and all the afternoons when she would lie in her yellow hammock between two locust trees which were hidden from the porch of the hotel.

Although Katharine Faraday had never been thought decorative enough to become even a flower-girl before, she managed to follow six white uniformed groomsmen and six white-frocked and crimson-hatted bridesmaids up the aisle of Saint Michael's Church without once looking towards the box-pews she was passing, and nevertheless to arrive at the altar with the first version of the phrases in which she would tell Captain Edward Cabot just the point in the rehearsal when she had decided that no blood is blue enough to take the place of elementary education, and just the point in her progress up the aisle when she had decided that no blood is blue enough to take the place of cold cream, or even of curling irons. When she turned to face the white satin in which Sarah Rutledge was approaching Second Lieutenant Henry Simpson, and which Katharine Faraday did not think was worthy of being folded in blue tissue paper and preserved for Sarah Rutledge's ascension from Magnolia

Cemetery on the day of judgment, she was wondering if Captain Cabot was too remotely descended from the Cabots of Massachusetts to enjoy having her tell him that after three days of inspection Charleston did not seem an uncommonly patriotic or an uncommonly martial town, but that apparently its customs allowed a commission in the United States Army to take the place of a whole family tree, and that apparently the most highly placed Charlestonian girl could marry an army officer without even one grandfather who had signed his name to the Declaration of Independence —if only the officer had been born outside the boundaries of South Carolina. When she slipped her own bouquet of well-wired crimson roses into the crook of her left arm and took the bouquet of well-wired white roses which she supposed Sarah Rutledge would hardly have chosen except as public proof that ten years of residence in Atlanta had not given her a taste for flowers so hysterical as orchids or so High Church as lilies, she was wondering if Sarah Rutledge could be thinking of anything except the dreadful sounds which had come through the opening and closing door of

Mrs. Pinckney Rutledge's room on the night before Harriet Rutledge was born. When she turned back the veil which had sheltered all those ladies of the Rutledge family who had achieved weddings, and which had successfully drooped its leaves and roses between Sarah Rutledge's lack of timidity and the interest natural in a congregation of her relations, she was rewarded by a remarkably mature example of the gracious condescension a wedded wife smiles at a spinster. She realised then that she had suffered a defeat more damaging than the defeat she suffered on the day Sarah Rutledge became a woman, and that no matter how many babies and no matter how many other calamities she might fear her union with Henry Simpson would bring her, Sarah Rutledge was triumphant in the realization that she was married. Katharine Faraday had not forgotten the afternoons and the nights when she had planned the yellow chiffon frocks and the yellow-plumed hats behind which she would walk down the aisle of the First Presbyterian Church beside the yellow stripes of the United States cavalry, but she did not regret the August night when she decided that she could never again endure the suspense of waiting for the miracle of a letter from James Fuller, and that she could not endure the possibility of his suspecting her of wanting to marry him if he did not want to marry her, and that she could never answer the letter which had escaped a thousand miles of dangers and which was pressed against the spot that was no longer tender and that was rose and yellow instead of blue. But when she laid her left hand against Captain Cabot's white sleeve —just as much more lightly than propriety demanded as Eleanor Faraday's experienced instruction specified—and told him she was sure he must have noticed how perfectly Sarah Rutledge's smile echoed Mendelssohn's triumphant nuptial waterfall, she regretted that neither propriety nor loyalty, nor Eleanor Faraday's instruction about hiding her more elaborate mental processes, allowed her to tell him she was sure he could not have guided so many bridegrooms to altars without wondering how Mendelssohn's chords managed to dash down half an organ, and nevertheless to shout out a pride of achievement exactly as triumphant as the pride a hen manages to convey in an ascending stutter. When she was arranging Sarah Rutledge's two yards of shining satin in a curve she had admired in a large flat magazine called The Spur, she was too much annoyed by Caroline Rutledge's interest in Captain Cabot's sword to find any conversational inspiration in the celebrated white marble mantel which Sarah Rutledge's maternal grandmother considered a fitting background for brides and for coffins. And when she sat down beside Captain Cabot on the lowest step of the piazza which looked down on the garden and on the little orange-tree which provided Sarah Rutledge's grandmother with one of the smaller reasons for a complacence that was noticeable even in Charleston, Katharine Faraday did not remember that she owed a satisfactory back-drop to a gentleman who was confidently awaiting a glorious resurrection on the left side of Saint Michael's churchyard. Neither did she realize that this James Monroe back-drop was set for the third act of the play which had begun beside the tall rubber-tree in the drawing room of the West Point Hotel, or that Edward Cabot was playing the part of the martial hero whose more youthful scenes had been played by James Fuller. But when Edward Cabot told her stories of the days when he was a yearling corporal and stories of the days when he had left West Point too late for the Spanish but in plenty of time for the Filipinos, she listened with an attention as visible as if she were not engaged in laying the memory of Sarah Rutledge's triumphant smile beside the memory that Henry Simpson was a second lieutenant and that Edward Cabot was captain of his battery. When the sunlight left the orange-tree which was not identified by oranges or by orange-blossoms, but which was a nicely symbolical proscenium arch, she enjoyed feeling cool enough to be wrapped in the martial cape which Edward Cabot proved his experience by turning on its crimson side. And she enjoyed the public isolation of a darkness she did not think about as a screen for the possible touch of Edward Cabot's experienced hand. When the attentions a maid of honour must show her bride obliged her to walk up the celebrated stairway which was another of the smaller reasons for the complacence of Sarah Rutledge's grandmother, Katharine Faraday was entirely occupied in wondering if Edward Cabot would really come over to Atlanta and dance with her in her white débutante's frock. But when she ran down the celebrated stairway with her red rosebud of rice, she had not forgotten the little grey box Sarah Rutledge had laid in her bag beside her bridal nightgown and her bridal negligé, and she had not forgotten Sarah Rutledge's assurance that it would delay the advent of Rutledge Simpson until he could be born in the quarters of a first lieutenant.

On the third Wednesday afternoon in November, Katharine Faraday dressed herself in a white crêpe de chine frock which had been made in Atlanta, and in which she was officially introduced to all those ladies whom she already knew and who could reasonably be expected to ask the right kind of young men to sit beside her at dinner or to sit behind her in theatre and opera boxes during the uncomfortable years when she would be professionally engaged in looking about for a husband, and in which she was also introduced to those ladies who could only be expected to ask her to lunch and to play bridge with girls who might ask her to dinner. On the third Wednesday evening in November, her mother and her mammy and her two sisters helped her into a white chiffon frock which had been made in Baltimore, and in which she was introduced to all those members of the Piedmont Driving Club whom she already knew and whose fathers had not worn policemen's uniforms or presided over their own greengroceries or lived over their own lime-kilns within the tenacious memory of Katharine Faraday's mother, and whose uncles had always been saved from the consequences of their misappropriations by the influence of their families. She was also introduced to an aging, wasting and presumably virgin spinster, whose gift for rolling saplings so loudly that she seemed to be rolling logs would probably have made her a cardinal if she had not suffered the misfortune of being born a woman, and whose descriptions of dinners and dances and weddings filled such elaborately bound scrap-books that she had attained every social honour except marriage. But since Katharine Faraday knew that journalists who described dances were not yet allowed the pleasure of choosing any of their adjectives on the impolite side of the pages which journalists who described plays seemed to memorize in the newer editions of Roget's thesaurus, she knew that Edward Cabot would be provided with a satisfactory description of her white chiffon frock and her crimson roses and her brunette beauty, and she allowed her failure to ask for breakfast on the morning of the third Thursday in November to suggest that she was still asleep. She lay in the bird's-eye maple bed in the pink room to which she always retired before the arrival of a visitor, and she thought about Edward Cabot's beautifully brushed yellow hair and his attentive blue eyes, and about the hours when she had sat beside him on the terrace instead of using the strategic advantage of her own début dance against a young lawyer who was called Neal Lumpkin as evidence that he was sure to get on in the world, and against a young man who was called Grant Jordan as evidence that his father had made too many paper bags for him to have any occasion to get on in the world. She thought about Edward Cabot's remarkable resemblance to the golden-haired tenor who was so tall and so fair that he was not likely to sing in the Metropolitan Opera House, but whom she had first seen in the white uniform of Lieutenant Pinkerton, and she wondered if the resemblance and the white uniform could possibly mean that she was ever likely to spend such a night of suspense as the night Madame Butterfly had very naturally failed to survive when such depressing music and the observation of a contralto were added to her natural anxiety. But when she found herself unable to stop wondering if Edward Cabot's legs could be like the legs her father still revealed by continuing to follow the strange custom which stopped nocturnal masculine costumes at the knee, and if he could be modelled precisely like George Faraday and the clear illustrations in Gray's Anatomy, she decided that the laws of hospitality would not allow her to put off knocking on the door of the blue room in which Isabel Ambler was presumably having her coffee. Katharine Faraday thought that a taste for coffee was evidence of an upbringing unbecoming an Ambler, and although she had never questioned the beauty of the nineteenth-century bed on which Isabel Ambler was lying between two of Mrs. Alexander Faraday's four linen sheets, she had never slept soundly on it since the day when she had learned that it was the birthplace of her mother and of her mother's six brothers and three sisters. But she sat down on it and leaned against one of the rosewood posts which might have been intended to support the ceiling instead of the blue satin tester that had once been the gown in which Marian Faraday first led a cotillion. And then she politely set about her belated duty of congratulating Isabel Ambler on her public conquest of a thin young man who was called Grantland Lamar as evidence that his grandfathers had both shed blood of the best quality on the red clay of half the counties to which their grandfathers had given their names, but that one of his great-grandfathers had known better than to buy any of the bonds printed by the Confederate States of America. She knew that Isabel Ambler would enjoy her congratulations, but that she would feel obliged to answer them by talking about the sufferings she had endured on Sunday morning when she had not been able to start for Saint Paul's Church at ten o'clock and stop to lay eighteen pink carnations on her lost Harrison's perfectly kept grave in Hollywood Cemetery. She also knew that the customs of Richmond do not require politeness of a girl whose great-grandmother had proved herself its ideal of southern womanhood by combining a degree of beauty which charmed George Washington with a degree of intelligence which refused the hand of George Washington. And since she did not know herself that she was entirely faithful to the martial hero of Katharine Faraday's second romantic tragedy and that Edward Cabot was only playing the rôle of the hero in the third act of the drama whose first two acts had been played by James Fuller, she was not surprised when Isabel Ambler's ideas of politeness did not require her to congratulate Katharine Faraday on an admirer who had remembered to bring his crimson-lined cape all the way from Fort Moultrie, and who had remembered to turn it on its crimson side when he wrapped it around her white chiffon frock before he sat down beside her in a white vest of which even George Faraday had not been able to disapprove. And since Edward Cabot was thirty-three years old, he had not made the mistake of mentioning Isabel Ambler's red hair or her white neck, and Katharine Faraday was not wishing for revenge when she began to admire the rose-coloured velvet in which she thought that Isabel Ambler looked like a young mother who was doing her duty by her children. But on the evening of the third Thursday in November, Katharine Faraday did not think of her own white lace between Isabel Ambler's rose-coloured velvet and Nellie Clark's apple-green satin, and she did not think about the play, which was called King Lear, or about its celebrated interpreter, who was called Robert Mantell, and she was not distressed because the audience was not made up of people who would realize that Katharine Faraday was sitting in the third box on the right side of the Grand Opera House. She was not thinking of anything except that she would not see Edward Cabot again until she went down to Sullivan's Island in January and stayed with Sarah Rutledge for the first Saint Cecilia Ball, and that she must look at his beautifully brushed hair and his blue eyes as often as she could before the terrible minute she would have to live through when a door closed behind him, and which she knew would be so coldly different from the minute before when he was still in the same room with her.

If journalistic custom had allowed chroniclers of dances to print the verdict of the experienced jury whom Mrs. Alexander Faraday had invited to inspect her youngest daughter on the third Wednesday in November, Atlanta would probably have read in the public prints of the third Thursday in November that Katharine Faraday's beauty would not be the occasion of increased civic pride which Eleanor Faraday's golden beauty had been for ten years, and that her dancing would never inspire orchestra leaders as Marian Faraday's dancing was still inspiring them after three years of unsatisfactory marriage. If journalistic custom had allowed the experienced spinster to print a reasoned review of Katharine Faraday instead of a polite description of Katharine Faraday's début dance, the conclusion of the sagacity which had won every social honour except marriage would almost certainly have been that Katharine Faraday's conversation was not interesting to her and that it was not likely to be interesting to the members of the Piedmont Driving Club, or even to the decreasingly important members of the Capital City Club, and that it was therefore not interesting. If Katharine Faraday had been privileged to hear the verdict which was spoken so often that it did not need to be printed except for her own enlightenment, she would not have been able to console herself with the realisation that interest is a completely transitive verb. But during her first official week of dinners and dances and theatres and Sunday afternoon callers, she discovered that she was less interesting to the members of the Piedmont Driving Club than she had been to the young men who came to Mrs. Randolph's dances and the young men who came to Mrs. Rutherford Cobb's dinners and the young men who came to West Point Hops. She gave herself up for lost on the evening when she realized that she could usually keep herself from talking to them about the things in which her mother said they could not possibly be interested, but that she could not give up thinking about Edward Cabot long enough to think up amusing remarks about the things they might be interested in. Whenever she opened an envelope which had already shot its blazing disappointment through her eyes down her whole body as she saw that it was not addressed by Edward Cabot or even postmarked in Fort Moultrie, and when she read a card which invited her to another dance, she felt a terror of anticipation she would not have felt if her dentist had set his awful chair in the midst of Peachtree Street and invited her world to stop and see how Katharine Faraday supported his borings. And when she was provided with the member of the Piedmont Driving Club without whom she could not walk into a ballroom as respectably as she could have walked in without two stockings, she knew her world must realize that she would not go to dances unless she wanted to be danced with, but she knew she could not walk away as she had walked away from the line of children in the Calhoun Street School's yard before they could discover that she might not have received the tap on the head which would have made her eligible to play Prisoner's Base. When she lay down on the nineteenth-century bed for the hour's sleep her mother considered the best beautifier for a ball-room, she always felt that she could not leave even that bed's depressing shelter for a room she knew would seem very cold. But the prospect of an awakening which might follow a victorious evening always made her slip into the white chiffon frock around which Edward Cabot had wrapped his cape, or into the crimson crêpe de chine shirred with gold threads or into the yellow crêpe satin he had never seen, and then go out and try to talk to men who did not seem to know that she had been tingling with radiance half an hour before, but whom she must please if she hoped to check off safely partnered dances as convicts may check off days without lashes. She had never suspected that men choose their partners for anything except pretty faces and pretty frocks and obedient dancing and the right conversation and the right quantity and volume of laughter, and when she smiled up at a young man with a smile which only meant that she wanted him to dance with her again, the answering pressure of his left arm was the first confirmation of her suspicion that membership in the Piedmont Driving Club was not a complete social reference, and to a new fear that she would always appeal to the wrong kind of man. But when a newspaper left all its other pages blank by failing to mention the town of Charleston or the artillery of the United States, she still saw announcements that the Atlanta Theatre or the Grand Opera House would shortly present a celebrated actor in an unsuccessful play or a successful play without any celebrated actor. She still remembered that her world would be waiting to see whether she walked into the play's first performance with one of the Piedmont Driving Club's younger members, and she began to listen for a ringing telephone as soon as she had stopped listening for the postman who would leave her whole body burning from the blazing fall of her disappointment, or who would leave it an alabaster lamp for the rising and falling glow of its electric spray.

When Katharine Faraday had carefully settled the little blue poke-bonnet and the two curves of black hair which Edward Cabot might just possibly be seeing in another fifteen minutes, she slipped on the short blue coat and the black fox he might also be seeing, and then she took up Eleanor Faraday's discarded bag and walked out to the green velvet seat which had been lower berth number twelve when she had left it half an hour before. She looked out of her window at the brown marshes which would gradually become the cobbled streets of Charleston, and she thought again that they looked like the taste of the tonic which her mother's doctor said was sure to increase her vitality, and which she hoped would increase her capacity for laughing at the anecdotes of the Piedmont Driving Club's members. She also thought of her unhappiness on the October afternoon when she had looked out at the brown marshes after the complacence of Sarah Rutledge's grandmother had made immediate separation from Edward Cabot preferable to another breakfast spent in trying not to see red pepper and yellow fish roe stirred into fine hominy, and in trying not to hear personal narratives of triumphs over those Charlestonian members of the Society of Colonial Dames of America whose ancestors were nothing more than respectable Huguenots. She opened the same little blue bag in which she had laid James Fuller's first card, and she took out the letter she had slipped under her thick pillow as soon as Neal Lumpkin had conformed with the requirements of gallantry by jumping off her train just after it had emerged from the squalor of the Union Station. Before she began to read the letter again, she remembered the relief of knowing that she was leaving Atlanta and the telephone which might not ring, and that five hundred Parma violets were pinned on her blue coat, and that she had not been escorted to the Union Station by one of her brothers, and that a copy of Life and a copy of Vogue and a copy of the Theatre Magazine and a silver and rose box of Page and Shaw's chocolates were lying beside the rustling bag which was protecting her blue poke-bonnet from the Georgia Railroad's cinders. Before she finished reading the letter, she began to think of the martial and therefore unanswerable arguments she would give Edward Cabot the pleasure of repeating when she told him about the strange old man who had sat behind her and Neal Lumpkin in the Atlanta Theatre the week before, and who had expressed the strange idea that no country ought to have a standing army. But she had read several hundred novels in which long silences were the overtures to proposals, and she wanted to spend the mornings of her second week in discussing chemises and petticoats and nightgowns and the correct conduct of bridal nights with Sarah Rutledge. By the time she saw the white spire of Saint Michael's Church, she had remembered that a silence of several minutes preceded Mr. Darcy's first proposal to Elizabeth Bennet and that a short pause preceded even his second proposal. And when she remembered that Jane Austen had never proved the reception of a proposal by an engagement, she was able to remember that Benjamin Disraeli had certainly made at least one proposal, and that his young duke stood beside May Dacre in silence before he offered her his fallen fortunes and then received her embrace. She decided that she would sit beside Edward Cabot in silence, and then she opened her blue bag again and powdered her small replica of her father's southern statesman nose more carefully than she would have powdered it for the inspection of any man except Captain Edward Cabot or the Right Honourable Arthur James Balfour. But she did not really expect the miracle of Edward Cabot's yellow hair and his blue uniform and his crimson stripes and his two silver bars beyond the brown and black bags of her twenty-five fellow passengers, and she was not astonished when she saw only the sawdust hair and the blue uniform and the crimson stripes and the empty shoulder straps of Second Lieutenant Henry Simpson. Henry Simpson explained his captain's absence with the illness of one first lieutenant and one major, and he explained his wife's absence with a reticence so conscious that Katharine Faraday remembered the day when Sarah Rutledge had not been able to wade in the stream beside which Saint Luke's Sunday School had picnicked. She tried to converse with Henry Simpson in the manner which was not any more successful with her satisfactory brother-in-law than it was with her unsatisfactory brother-in-law, but which seemed to be the correct manner for a bridegroom whose bride's bouquet she had held, and whose captain had written the letter against which her left hand was lying in her blue bag. Henry Simpson accepted her uninteresting conversation with a deference which seemed to suggest a conviction that she might shortly become an important person in his world, and she was already beginning to tingle with radiance before the little boat came so near Sullivan's Island that she could see Edward Cabot's yellow hair above the crimson lining of the cape which was blown back by the cold fishy wind. She was sure that she would have been absolutely happy if the proprieties of accepting hospitality had allowed her to say that she did not want to stand in the wind and risk a red nose, or even if the proprieties of nineteen hundred and twelve had allowed public powdering. But she had just discovered that propriety allowed her to slip her grey glove off her right hand, and when she put it into Edward Cabot's hand she felt that their reunion was a miracle almost as supernatural as Edward Cabot's existence. When she went up to the cold bedroom from which Sarah Rutledge did not feel able to come down to greet a guest with whom she had drunk rusty water at the Calhoun Street School, Katharine Faraday was not annoyed by Sarah Rutledge's conscious reticence about the illness which had not allowed her to cross the harbour, but which would certainly allow her to take Katharine Faraday out to play bridge in the afternoon, and to the Saint Cecilia Society's ball on Thursday evening. She was not annoyed even when the illness allowed Sarah Rutledge to say that the crimson crêpe de chine shirred with gold threads would probably displease the society's president and its managers and their wives, even though Edward Cabot had never seen Katharine Faraday in crimson. And when Sarah Rutledge felt able to say that if Katharine Faraday should feel an interest in any young gentleman which led her to think of going outside the ball-room door to the secluded stairway of the Hibernian Hall, she would do well to remember the fate of the young woman who had once gone out of the door and whose increasing consequence at Newport and on Fifth Avenue had never allowed her to walk back through it, Katharine Faraday was not interested in anything except getting a better light on the mirror in which she was looking at the colour of the face Edward Cabot had just seen.

When Katharine Faraday walked into the ball-room of the Hibernian Hall behind the white satin in which Sarah Rutledge was making her last public entry before the day of judgment, she felt as if she were about to take an examination in the rules of the Saint Cecilia Society. But she was consoled by the certainty that she was walking into a ball-room where there could not be any young men of the wrong kind, and she was reconciled to the rules of the society when she found that they required an invitation to dance and a signed contract on a card of every young man who was introduced to her. She was able to look away from Edward Cabot long enough to see that a great many young gentlemen and young ladies of the right kind had eyes like pale hot water and faces like dull oak frames, and that when they were circling the ball-room together between the somewhat stately dances, they looked exactly like an unpatronised merry-go-round in the country of the

Houyhnhnms. She was distressed that the rules of the society required its ladies to wear their best gowns from the year before to its first ball and to keep their best new gowns for the second ball, and she was distressed that the rules did not allow Edward Cabot to sit down beside her at supper and that she was expected to enjoy eating rice at midnight. But she was pleased when they allowed at least one glass of champagne to a débutante in a white lace frock and silver-wreathed hair, and when the greatly decreased stateliness of the after-supper dancing suggested that they allowed even the right kind of young gentlemen half a dozen glasses. She realized that a Saint Cecilia dance-card was harder to come by than a programme of Parsifal and that it would be an enviable ornament of her big book. But when she smiled up at Edward Cabot, she had some reason to think that she felt an answering pressure of his left arm, and she was not sorry when Sarah Rutledge found that terrapin and champagne had been a mistake and when the impossibility of remaining in the Hibernian Hall without a chaperon allowed her to go back to Sullivan's Island with the consolation of remembering that even if Edward Cabot had wanted to ask her to marry him, Sarah Rutledge and the rules of the society had not allowed him the seclusion and the silence which seemed to be necessary. When she went down to the drawing-room the next morning, she wanted an exclusively feminine audience for her dream about the odd things James Fuller had said to her on a white marble balcony, and she was glad that Sarah Rutledge came in as she was settling the angle of the aigrette on the geranium coloured straw hat in which she was about to walk out among the palmettoes and the sand dunes with Edward Cabot. But she was sorry that Sarah Rutledge's sickness had suddenly compelled the end of her reticence, and that she chose those ten minutes for her annunciation of the probable reasons why the contents of the little grey box she had slipped into the bag with her bridal night-gown had not prevented the probability that Rutledge Simpson would be born in a second lieutenant's quarters in July. Katharine Faraday knew that Sarah Rutledge could not allow even a daughter to be born out of South Carolina, even though her father's house in

Atlanta was likely to be cooler in July than Sullivan's Island, and she offered something which she thought was a tactful combination of congratulation and condolence without looking at Sarah Rutledge directly enough to receive the brave smile a prospective mother would doubtless be able to give a spinster even in the unpleasant hours of the morning. When Edward Cabot's arrival had proved the error of Katharine Faraday's belief that something would certainly keep him from coming for her, Katharine Faraday was able to tell him about her discovery that captains were always tall and slim, but that apparently they always became short and fat on the day they were commissioned majors and then became tall and thin on the day they were commissioned lieutenant-colonels. And when he became convinced that she was tired as soon as they had rounded a remote and secluded dune, she was able to sit down in the silence which should be the overture to a proposal. When Edward Cabot dropped his blue cap on the sand and stood up in front of her, she was able to look up at him and to smile a smile which meant that he had yellow hair and blue eyes, and that she was tingling with the radiance of an emotion she did not doubt was love and with the necessity of hiding it until a human being who could not have a baby asked affection from a human being who probably could have a baby. Katharine Faraday had read several hundred novels in which proposals addressed to heroines without fortunes were the result of affection, but she had never gathered that they are usually the result of emotion, and she did not suspect that Edward Cabot might possibly be dropping into that emotion when he caught off her geranium hat with one hand and caught her against his blue coat with the other. She knew that if Edward Cabot could offer her the insult of an unbetrothed kiss he did not love her, and in less than an hour Mrs. Alexander Faraday had read a telegram which annoyed her by announcing that Sarah Rutledge was very ill and that Katharine Faraday would arrive at the Union Station the next morning.

When Katharine Faraday had spent two days in listening for the ringing of a telephone which she had not meant to hear for another ten days and in watching for a postman who did not bring her anything except invitations, and two nights in dreaming that she would certainly meet Edward Cabot around the next curve of the Hudson River, she put on the little blue poke-bonnet which brought back such a blemishing memory of the dock at Sullivan's Island that she felt as if she were standing in front of her mirror to adjust an unbecoming crown of thorns. But Eleanor Faraday's husband would not have thought of choosing any street except Peachtree Street for the beamed brick and plaster house which he had built as a golden frame for Eleanor Faraday's celebrated golden beauty, and which he considered a satisfactory improvement on a celebrated Warwickshire country-seat. And although Katharine Faraday had not yet brought herself to open the box which still held the geranium straw hat with the aigrette, she found a lining of memorial thistles less painful than the idea of walking down Peachtree Street in one of the felt and velvet hats which the customs of Atlanta sent to its attics or to its cooks and maids before New Year's Day. She did not intend to tell her satisfactorily married sister that she had wanted Edward Cabot to ask her to marry him in April, but the conversation of her family had led her to believe that no living woman except Mrs. Grover Cleveland combined beauty with all Eleanor Faraday's social subtleties. And since she could not look up the meaning of an unbetrothed kiss in any other social dictionary she thought equally reliable, she wanted to look up a purely theoretical problem in a triumphant experience which covered all the important towns and all the important dances and all the important men of ten southern states, and some of the important dances and some of the important men of Washington and New York and even Philadelphia. But Katharine Faraday's confidence in her family's conversation was a good deal diminished by Eleanor Faraday's failure to answer her theoretical questions with the black and white neutrality she had expected to find in such a well-bred dictionary of love. She ran down her brother-in-law's cedar bordered stone steps while she was thinking that Mrs. Grover Cleveland could never have been so untactfully unkind, and that if Eleanor Faraday had been born in Charleston and on Legaré Street, she could hardly have spoken less politely about the damaging effects of Katharine Faraday's entirely unconcealed affection for Edward Cabot. But she could not think of Eleanor Faraday's suggestion that Katharine Faraday should write Edward Cabot a calm little note in which she might tell him that she did not want their pleasant friendship to end so uncomfortably and that she hoped he could give her a reason which would allow her to forget the things that had happened three days before. She walked down Peachtree Street while she was hoping that Eleanor Faraday's baby would give her at least three extremely painful days and nights when it gave up defying matrimonial and medical calculations and consented to be born, and while she was hoping that it would be a girl and that it would grow up extremely ugly and that Eleanor Faraday would rise from her Sheraton bed with that loose-haired milky look which usually identified young mothers as certainly as the cut of their navy blue taffeta frocks. But before she ran up her father's green wooden steps, she had decided that even Eleanor Faraday's journalistic advice was not as bad as submissive endurance of suspense, and that with the one exception of the verb murder, she would rather be the subject of any verb than its passive object. And since she did not want to wake up at dawn wondering if a postman had lost her letter out of his open bag, she walked down to the post-office and then read over the address three times before she dropped it through the appointed bronze slit. Every night for two weeks, she dreamed that she was reading a very long and very satisfactory letter from Edward Cabot and every day for two weeks she accepted all her invitations so that she could not be waiting at home for the postman, and every time she came back into the dark oak hall, she looked for a long white envelope between the two silver candlesticks on the table she did not know was a Duncan Phyfe table. But Edward Cabot did not write her the letter in which she wanted him to say that he had been obliged to kiss her because he loved her, and that when she ran away from him he had been about to beg her to marry him in April, and that he had been sure her flight had been meant to spare him the pain of a more verbal refusal. One week after she decided that the story of Katharine Faraday and Edward Cabot was complete, she was able to put on the geranium straw hat, and she was able to forget all her dreams before she woke. And although she had not begun to doubt that she had ever been in love with Edward Cabot, she was able to write Blanche Richardson that she would be delighted to come down to New Orleans for Mardi Gras week, and that if Tony Richardson really liked her photograph so much that he wanted her flowers to be exactly right, Blanche Richardson could tell him that her visitor would be going to the Carnival German in a crimson crêpe de chine shirred with gold threads. Before she had walked up the steps of the New York and New Orleans Limited, she had done a good deal for her wounded pride by constant applications of the idea that she would never have to be sure wounded affection had not kept Edward Cabot from answering her letter. She was able to lie down beside a thick pillow without any letter under it, and to nestle against her own cleverness in realising already that when a girl is in one town and a man is in another town, the door between them is locked on her side as long as the girl has an unanswered letter under her pillow, and that she was now too experienced ever to make the mistake she had made when she took Eleanor Faraday's stupid advice and wrote Edward Cabot the calm little note which allowed him to keep the door locked on his side.

Since Arthur Faraday was sure men would never publicly admit that they had seen their best days by inviting women into the polls women had nothing at all to do with inventing, and since he did not think Katharine Faraday was likely to charm votes out of his enemies, he never conversed with his youngest sister. And since he spent all his mornings and all his afternoons in walking from the offices where George Faraday was searching out legal precedents for their clients' civil and criminal misfortunes to the offices of other lawyers and other political headquarters, and all his evenings at political meetings and political dinners where white vests were not required, Katharine Faraday had never thought about him except during the week when she wondered why a man who wanted to become ambassador to the Court of Saint James should have begun by getting himself elected something he called commissioner of Fulton County, and whether there would be anything very triumphant about being presented to King George the Fifth as the sister of an ambassador. He became a character in her own story of her own life on the Mardi Gras morning which followed her successful collecting of little fans and little powder-boxes and lily strung fish-nets at the Carnival German, and her distress when she drank two glasses of champagne at Antoine's Restaurant and then found that it did not improve her conversation while she was dancing with the alarmingly dressed and discouragingly masked Krewe of Proteus. While she was hooking the Alice blue ratiné frock which had been an afternoon frock in Atlanta but which Blanche Richardson said was the correct frock for a morning spent in sitting on the Boston Club's balcony behind the queen of the carnival, and in looking down with her on her brocaded king and his passing courtiers and on the people who did not seem sufficiently depressed by their ineligibility for the Boston Club's balcony, she stopped to take a telegram from the silver salver of the butler whose dark and aged elegance might easily have been Blanche Richardson's compensation for the inelegance of her father. While she was tearing the envelope, she was telling herself hopefully that it could not possibly be from Edward Cabot, although her pride had forced her to write Sarah Rutledge that she was going down to New Orleans for Mardi Gras, and to mention Blanche Richardson's satisfactory address. But when she saw her father's name on the last line of the telegram, she was disappointed enough to be able to burst into tears as soon as she saw that Arthur Faraday was very ill and that her father wanted her to come back to Atlanta on the first train in which she could get a berth with one of the larger numbers. When Katharine Faraday was unhooking her ratiné frock, she did not regret Tony Richardson and the other members of the Mystic Krewe of Comus who might have danced with her in the evening. But she regretted the existence of a god who could look down through the top of an all steel Pullman and through her blue poke-bonnet and through all her black hair into a brain which would be hoping that Arthur Faraday would die and save her from the necessity of going to any more dances.

When Katharine Faraday walked past a long sheaf of white roses and into the dark oak hall, so many letters and cards and telegrams were lying between the two silver candlesticks that a glance could not settle the presence of her own name on anything except an invitation. And a wide acquaintance with the best bred English fiction had taught her that a lack of interest in letters is part of the etiquette of bereavement. It had also taught her that society does not seem to be nearly so sceptical about sorrowing affection for a deceased brother as it is about sorrowing affection for a deceased husband, and that it does not require a sister to give such expensive sartorial proofs of her distress as it requires from the partner of the victim's bed. But she knew that her blue poke-bonnet and her geranium straw hat were now as indecorous covering as a night-cap, and she knew that the etiquette of bereavement would not allow her to descend even to the first floor of her father's house until the moment when it would oblige her to put on a black hat which could not be made of straw, and to follow Arthur Faraday's mortal remains out to West View Cemetery. Her speculations on the possibility that her bereavement might end Edward Cabot's proud silence did not keep her from remembering the hats in which she had seen her Presbyterian aunt's two obliging daughters and the hats in which she had seen George Faraday's prospective bride. And her memories of those hats did not allow her to hope that any of them could choose a black hat in which she could possibly walk down Peachtree Street when the passage of a month allowed her to make an appearance public enough to settle the question of how she looked in a black taffeta hat and a black crêpe de chine frock with a white ruching around its modest neck and its even more modest sleeves. Her observations had convinced her that girls in their nineteenth year are the only good judges of hats, although younger girls and older women sometimes seemed to know a good hat when they saw it on the head of the nineteen year old girl who had been clever enough to choose it. But when propriety allowed her to receive Nellie Clark and Nellie Clark's offers of unlimited assistance, she knew that she could not have brought herself to choose a hat which was likely to increase the charms of such a contemporary rival for the favour of the younger members of the Piedmont Driving Club. And when George Faraday's prospective bride obligingly brought her the hat in which her own younger sister had completed her public regret for her mother's death, Katharine Faraday decided to follow Arthur Faraday to his grave in a last year's Crocker hat instead of trusting an intimate friendship which was founded on nothing more than the convenience of liking a girl who had found favour in the eyes of the most intimate friend of a young man who liked Katharine Faraday's grey eyes and her conversation, and on the afternoon when Nellie Clark had ladled a potent punch into little glass cups at Katharine Faraday's début tea and the immediately preceding afternoon when Katharine Faraday had ladled a less potent punch into the same little glass cups at Nellie Clark's début tea. When Grant Jordan sent her an elegiac box of gardenias on the morning after Arthur Faraday's funeral and Neal Lumpkin sent her a book written by a man called Henry Drummond, consolingly called Eternal Life and consolingly bound in purple suède, she was convinced that the enduring correctness of the hat's lines must have been visible even through the veil in which George Faraday's prospective bride had begun her own public regret for her mother. And she did not seriously regret her economical decision even when George Faraday allowed himself the impropriety of sitting down on the very edge of the nineteenth-century bed on which Katharine Faraday was allowing herself the impropriety of lying in the blue negligé which had not yet been dyed a permissibly blue shade of purple, and combined his legal manner with his brotherly manner while he told her that Arthur Faraday's estate would probably be something like ten thousand dollars, and that Arthur Faraday had left all of it to her. She was glad that she was able to cry, and that she had been able to cry more than her father or her mother or any of Arthur Faraday's four other brothers and sisters. And her pleasure in such a surprising proof of Arthur Faraday's surprising ability to appreciate her uncommon charms was not disturbed by any suspicion that the gift for understanding his fellow men which had made him Fulton County's youngest commissioner had convinced him that his youngest sister would never have the kind of charms which were likely to get her a satisfactory husband, or which were likely to get her any husband at all.

Katharine Faraday provided herself with two black frocks which she thought were suited to a girl who had just inherited an income of something less than fifty-five dollars a month, and with two black hats which were the cause of her fondness for saying that if their price-marks were fastened outside their crowns, a twenty-five dollar hat could not be more easily distinguished from a ten dollar hat. But she did not suspect that her lack of confidence in her world's ability to appreciate her charms had been pleasantly diminished by her belief that Arthur Faraday had been able to appreciate them, and she did not suspect that if Arthur Faraday had divided his ten thousand dollar estate equally between his three sisters, she would still have been afraid that her own charms would be overshadowed by the charms of those hats and those frocks. And since she did not suspect that her affection for Arthur Faraday had never existed and that no amount of multiplying could increase it, she was distressed when the etiquette of inheritance could not keep her from speculating about the strange circumstance that Arthur Faraday had apparently died without having any good reason for dying. When she asked them well-bred questions, Marian and Eleanor Faraday retreated either into their grief or into their wedded dignity. When she turned to the public prints, she found that The Atlanta Journal and The Atlanta Georgian and The Atlanta Constitution had successively recognised Arthur Faraday's social and political importance by depriving Woodrow Wilson of the column on their front pages which was filled with Arthur Faraday's genealogical and biographical achievements, but that those newspapers' most highly paid neocrologists apparently had not known the cause of the untimely taking off which was such a serious loss to his city and his state and his country. When even her mammy persisted in saying that men so hard-hearted and so ignorant as doctors could not be expected to find out anything in three days, Katharine Faraday realised that she would have to cast about in her own excellent memory. In the course of a round dozen years interspersed with asking and receiving permissions, she was able to find memories of several afternoons when she had pushed back one of the blue curtains which usually formed her mother's drawing-room door, and when she had found herself walking into a conversation at the moment when her mother was hearing or saying that some unfortunate gentleman was suffering or dying or dead from a disease of a private nature. She was able to remember an afternoon which she had found very interesting when she was fifteen years old and when her newly achieved womanhood made her Presbyterian aunt's conversation agreeably alarming, and when she had stood outside the blue curtains long enough to hear the distressing history of a young woman who had been born in a town called Omaha and who did not know how to cook rice, and who had nevertheless grown tired of teaching girls something which she called domestic science, but which did not seem to be anything more than broiling chops and folding napkins. Katharine Faraday also remembered how long she had waited before she had heard that the tired young woman had refused to believe the detailed warnings Katharine Faraday's aunt had been able to give her against the only man who wanted to marry her, and that she was now lying in a bed of ice, and no farther away than Saint Joseph's Infirmary around the corner on Courtland Street. She remembered with some satisfaction that when she had waited long enough to hear about an unfortunate colored woman called Beulah, who had washed the clothes of the tired teacher's baby during its one week of existence, and who was now lying in the Henry Grady Hospital and presumably in a bed of ice, she had decided that her mother would rather have her go down to the Carnegie Library without permission than be discovered in the midst of a conversation so unbecoming a southern lady. And she was not ashamed of her fifteen year old self even when she remembered that she had walked down Courtland Street—although she was wearing her best hat—and that when she had told the tired teacher's story to Mildred Cobb as they walked slowly past Saint Joseph's Infirmary, they had been more interested in wondering if the nuns knew the exact causes of all their patients' diseases than they had been in deciding to change a story called The Princess Priscilla's Fortnight for an even older story called The Heart of the Princess Osra. She was a little mortified when she thought about the days when she had considered royal romances excellent preparation for a future which might possibly be spent at one court or another, but the memory of those literary researches suggested the idea of going down into the library and reading a little in the eleventh volume of the copy of Nelson's Encyclopedia whose purchase she put down to her father's unfortuante admiration for eloquence. When she found her mother answering letters of condolence in the library, she said that she was about to refresh her memory of the Smithsonian Institution in Washington, and she hoped that an interest in the earliest American mammals was not a violation of the etiquette of bereavement. When she walked back up the oak stairs ten minutes later, she was meditating on her discovery that the amorous Latin natures of Christopher Columbus's mariners had introduced Europe to a disease which did not actually follow the law of the sea far enough to respect the frailty of women and children, but which provided men with a consequence of polygamy and even of monogamy that seemed to be nearly as uncomfortable as a baby. And before she opened her own door, she had begun to feel that Christopher Columbus had probably justified the trouble he had taken to discover a hemisphere which apparently could not produce any books except books like Elsie Dinsmore and Ethan Frome.

When Arthur Faraday dropped a black veil between Katharine Faraday and her world, she was grateful for its temporary shelter. But she had listened to a great deal of conversation during the evenings when she had looked on at her sisters' careful preparations for dining and dancing, and she knew that in her world a girl who suffered a bereavement usually decided against returning to the competition of ball-rooms after she had lost a respectful year or two of her youthful bloom. She knew that these marriages were sometimes politely attributed to the endearing effect of sorrow and the beautifying effect of Crocker hats. But since her own bereavement had not ended Edward Cabot's proud silence, she preferred a theory that retirement from ball-rooms and drawing-rooms was likely to diminish their meetings with satisfactory young men, and that sensible girls usually settled on the least unsatisfactory young man who was available at the moment, and passed from the restful shelter of mourning directly into the restful shelter of marriage. She did not want to walk into the ball-room of the Piedmont Driving Club again until she could walk into it beside a satisfactory husband, and since she had never considered the possibility of not walking into it at all, she read Neal Lumpkin's limp purple copy of Eternal Life, and she tried to believe that his habit of walking on his toes was the result of living in a house with his sister and his sister's three babies, and that he would certainly recover from the habit during the completely childless year he would spend after his own wedding. During one of the evenings of conversation in the lamplight and the firelight which she supposed must help to make bereavement such a frequent prologue to marriage, she told him she did not think a girl should ever be married at all unless she was one of those girls who agreed with her mother that a woman's success is her husband's success, and she told him that she could not think of a more interesting life than a life spent in asking her husband's most influential friends and enemies to dinner and then providing them with irresistible birds and turkeys and irresistible conversation. She had overheard a conversation in which her father and her oldest brother agreed with Neal Lumpkin's sound masculine views, and with his wisdom in conducting his campaign for a seat in the Georgia legislature by making speeches against an opponent who wanted to raise something called the age of consent. She had also heard their agreement with the speeches which seemed to be polite elaborations of a theory that raising the age of consent meant increasing the possibility that perfectly respectable young Georgians—who might even be sons and grandsons of the heroes who wore the grey—would be hanged for nothing more than the violation of fourteen year old virgins. And since she was sure his speeches must be agreeable to audiences which she supposed were made up entirely of men whose chief pleasure in life was the violation of virgins, she would have liked to tell him why she was sure the approaching Democratic white primary would select him to represent Fulton County in the Georgia legislature. But she knew that in Georgia no lady was supposed to know she was a virgin until she had ceased to be one, and that she was supposed to find the adjective's application to Mary the mother of Jesus as mysterious as the incarnation and its application to Elizabeth as mysterious as the reasons why a royal lady with so many suitors had never taken a husband. For the first time, she realised that conversation might have been entirely satisfactory if women had been allowed to admit that they understood the limited number of subjects men were interested in, and she was so excited by her idea that she almost committed the social crime of allowing a conversation to pause. But she had decided that she did not see why Neal Lumpkin's political sagacity should not lead him from the Georgia legislature to the United States senate, or even to the large mahogany bed above which a golden eagle watched over dreaming presidents of the United States, and she recovered in time to tell him about the remarkable resemblance between his profile and the profile Gilbert Stuart painted of Thomas Jefferson. History had not yet proved that the wives of Democratic presidents are not invariably more charming than the wives of Republican presidents, and she ceased to regret Edward Cabot after she began to spend her first hour in bed arranging the conversation she thought would be suited to the charming wife of the third Democratic president after the Civil War. She did not doubt that she had been in love three times, and even in her earlier youth she had not been one of those people who believe that if a quotation has rhyme or metre it is legal and psychological evidence, but she began to doubt the correctness of her settled belief that no woman has ever loved unless she has loved at first sight.

Since Katharine Faraday had listened to so much experienced conversation, she knew that Neal Lumpkin might merely be spending economical and restful evenings with a girl who could not go to plays or operas or dances, and who could not even wear violets. But after two months of firelight and lamplight shining on the nineteenth-century sofa in her mother's blue drawing-room and one month of waxing and waning moonlight shining through the water oaks which hung over her father's green porch, she began to think that he was probably conducting a very slow courtship. And she began to think that the conversational opportunities of bereavement were annoyingly decreased by the necessity of echoing his confidence in all the faiths of his fathers which concerned God and women and negroes and cotton, and that the impossibility of contributing literary evidence against some of those faiths made an evening spent in his society something like a morning spent in suffering from the impossibility of rising to fill gaps in her minister's information. Even with such encouraging scenery, she had never felt the electric spray of her fountain after an evening with him, and she had not yet been able to enjoy imagining the heroic and touching endurance of her affection for him after he had his back broken in the hunting field, or after he had his eyes beautifully disfigured in some less elegant American substitute for pheasant shooting, and she began to fear that she would never be magnificently in love with him. But she knew that her immediately contemporary rivals found her black veil pleasantly transparent, and Arthur Faraday's public approval had not given her so much confidence in her world's ability to appreciate her charms that she dared to risk discarding a young man who was likely to sit in the United States senate even if he never slept in the presidential bed, and who would always be at least a member of the Nine O'Clock German Club. Even after the night when she was attacked and conquered by a suspicion that his confidence in the immediately adjacent past was more than likely to include confidence in nightshirts as unbecoming as her own father's, she was still able to listen for his telephone calls with interesting anxiety. And she was still so much concerned about the newspapers' announcements of well-bred engagements that she slipped into her purple negligé before eight o'clock every Sunday morning and braved three or four feet of her father's front porch, and then stood just inside the dark oak hall until she had read as far down the columns as any chronicler of engagements would place even the most ignominious engagement of a Lumpkin. She did not want to marry him as soon as propriety would allow her a wedding which could obey her mother's proclamation that women should always be married on the housetops, or even as soon as it would allow her a wedding which would impress all the masculine white Democrats who would be twenty-one years old in time to become his constituents. But only the impossibility of kissing him would have made her tell him that she did not want to marry him at all, and she was relieved when a very hot June allowed her to go away to North Carolina, and when the cautiousness of his judicial temperament and the calm politeness of her own attention, and her father's fondness for sitting on his porch and handing down political wisdom to promising young men, allowed her to go away with no more positive evidence of Neal Lumpkin's affection than the two brown volumes of Buckle's History of Civilization in England. She began to read the first volume with the interest she always felt in any book which was given to her by any man, and when she came to the relation between the large Irish potato crop and the large number of Irish babies, she was sure he had presented her with a skeleton key to all knowledge and all wisdom, and she was glad to remember his assurance that his father had presented Buckle to his bride as the basis of education for an enlightened statesman's wife.

In the summer of nineteen hundred and twelve, the etiquette of bereavement did not allow Katharine Faraday to sit down in the little hotel's carved oak parlours, or to sit down on its honeysuckle-hung porch long enough to admire one of the sunsets which are works of God, and which could be less publicly admired even during the first six months of mourning. But propriety had begun to admit that the loss of a brother and the inheritance of his estate do not take the place of fresh air and regular exercise, and even though the mushrooms were gathered to be cooked and eaten, it allowed her to walk out with her acquaintances in search of one kind of mushroom called rubescens and another kind called russelas. Only three days after Neal Lumpkin had jumped off her train just as it was leaving the Terminal Station, she walked through the rhododendron thicket which always depressed her because it was such an admirable setting for a romance, and in front of a tall green tree which would have looked like the tall rubber-tree in the West Point Hotel if it had not been covered with icy pink blossoms, the number of her acquaintances was increased by the presentation of a young man who was not quite tall enough or quite thin enough to be worthy of his backdrop. His name was nothing more historic than Henry Brown, and she was so sure her own mother could not have settled such a name in its correct state and city that she was not seriously annoyed when she was almost immediately presented to his wife. But ever since Marian Faraday's wedding-day, she had disliked married affection because it made her feel as mortifyingly lonely as she felt whenever she was not in love on a moonlit night. And when Henry Brown's wife laid a visibly engaged and wedded left hand on his shoulder, Katharine Faraday was very much annoyed —annoyed enough to wish she could forget propriety long enough to tell May Huger that if she had to walk through the rhododendron thicket with such an amorously ill-bred husband and wife, she would not be able to converse with them any more rationally than if she had been pushed into bed with them. But when she had walked behind him long enough to see that he did not lay his hand on his wife's shoulder and to hear his more recent biography from May Huger, she began to think that Henry Brown apparently had some regard for his dignity as an Oxonian and a lecturer on English literature in the University of South Carolina, and she began to enjoy suspecting that Mrs. Henry Brown was a good deal less charming than her husband had thought her before she became his bride during his Easter holiday. When she heard that he had written an article about an author called Thomas Love Peacock, and that the article had been published either in a periodical called The Yale Review or in an almost equally erudite periodical called The North American Review, she began to enjoy suspecting that he had probably been as much surprised when he found himself publicly engaged as the eligible young man who had almost certainly wanted to marry Eleanor Faraday, and who was commonly supposed to have fainted after he read in three newspapers that he was engaged to a girl whose beauty had never been the occasion of civic pride. Katharine Faraday had never conversed with a man who gave lectures about English literature, and American fiction still painted such respectful portraits of American professors that she had no reason to doubt either their erudition or their intelligence. And since she had never looked into either The Yale Review or The North American Review, she had no reason to doubt that all their authors were everything American authors can ever hope to be, and she liked the idea of becoming interesting to a man who had written something more notable than descriptions of funerals and football games and of legal and illegal executions. Even if she had not been sure that his publicly affectionate wife would be annoyed, she would have been pleased when the first volume of Buckle drew him to the violet and grey hammock which was the most plaintive hammock she had been able to buy with one-tenth of her June income, and which she had hung between the two locust trees that were not visible from the little hotel's porch. She knew that the men of her world ceased to be eligible as soon as they were legally married, and that since the girls of her world did not often think of being interested by the things which the necessity of being interesting made them talk about to men, no sensible girl ever damaged her fragile reputation by talking to a man through the bars of matrimony. But she could not resist the consoling ease of talking to a man who could not possibly suppose that she wanted him to ask her to marry him, and who could not possibly mortify her by interrupting a courtship with the announcement of his engagement to a girl who could hardly be as clever as she was. And she could not resist her conviction that a conversation between Katharine Faraday and a man who had written an article about Thomas Love Peacock might easily be as successful as any conversation in the plays of Henry Arthur Jones. When Henry Brown came back to converse with her during some of the mornings and afternoons and evenings when his wife was suffering from an illness which Katharine Faraday supposed was the same illness Sarah Rutledge was still suffering from, she enjoyed the idea that his wife was distressed by having him beyond tactile reach, and she enjoyed the idea that he liked the satisfaction of providing one side of a conversation she admired very much, and of listening to the other side. She was not distressed when she discovered that Henry Brown was more interested in her black hair and her grey eyes than he was in an audience for his opinions about the relative merits of Sir John Falstaff and Captain Bobadil. But she was surprised that she was obliged to act an outraged virtue she could not feel on the moonlit evening when he stood up and looked down at her while she sat on an uncomfortable bench and looked up at him with a smile which meant that she was excited because she was interesting to a published author even though he was only an American author. While she was walking quickly across the grass to the back door of her father's cottage, she was remembering that she must have smiled up at Edward Cabot very much as she had smiled up at Henry Brown, and she was feeling all the satisfaction of a scientific discovery because she realized how much her future life might be influenced by the knowledge that if a girl sits down and smiles up at a man who is looking down at her, he will certainly kiss her if he takes either an honourable or a dishonourable interest in her.

Katharine Faraday's mother had lived most of her well-bred life before gardening succeeded charity as the social ladder with the smoothest rungs, and before the conversation at lunches became so horticultural that she thought it would probably have been unintelligible to Peter Henderson himself. She thought that a taste for flowers was a necessary quality of all southern ladies, and that a moderate interest in large and brilliant blossoms was hardly less compatible with the other qualities of southern gentlemen than a taste for large dogs. But her admiration for flowers was so impersonal that it could not compete with her convictions about the necessity of paying off obligations and of incurring them, and only the expectation of guests within two days ever kept her from replacing the card in a box of flowers with her own card, or from readdressing it as soon as she had observed the name and the colour of the flowers she must mention in the note of thanks she always sat down to write as soon as she had sent the box away. She would not have considered diminishing visible evidence of her youngest daughter's attractions by allowing her to replace the card in the box of gardenias Grant Jordan sent on the morning of the twenty-first birthday he thought was a twentieth birthday. But even the most brunette southern beauties had given up wearing crimson roses in their hair, and when Katharine Faraday opened the box of crimson roses Neal Lumpkin had sent to welcome her back to Atlanta and to celebrate the birthday he also thought was a twentieth birthday, her mother told her that she would be foolishly wasteful if she watched them fade herself instead of taking them down to Sarah Rutledge and paying off a very small part of the great obligation she had incurred when she went to a Saint Cecilia Ball. Katharine Faraday put half a dozen of the roses in a tall silver vase as visible evidence to convince Neal Lumpkin that all his other roses were on her own dressing-table, and as visible evidence when Nellie Clark came in to talk about the impossibility of wearing her frocks and hats across the Atlantic Ocean on a boat which might easily be full of satisfactory men, and the impossibility of buying new hats and frocks which certainly could not be worn in Paris. And then she walked down Myrtle Street and dreaded the moment when Sarah Rutledge would welcome her with a mature example of the gracious thanks the mother of a son would be sure to smile at a spinster. She knew that Henry Simpson had come up to Atlanta to assist in displaying the little boy who was his son and who was also a Rutledge born on the soil of South Carolina and baptized at the font of Saint Michael's Church. But she had not prepared herself to see Henry Simpson looking at Rutledge Simpson as she supposed Napoleon Bonaparte looked at the little boy who was his son and who was also a Hapsburg born in the Palace of the Tuileries and baptized in the Cathedral of Notre Dame de Paris. And she had not prepared herself for the domestic scene she saw when Harriet Rutledge took her up to the hot room where Henry Simpson was standing in a striped shirt which she thought was very ugly, and where he was leaning over the nineteenth-century bed in which his wife and his son were proving that a mother and her child were not always as beautiful a sight as they seemed to have been in fifteenth-century Italy. Katharine Faraday had seen the word uxorious in several of the novels her mother did not know she had read, but she knew that she was just realising what it meant. And when she had admired Rutledge Simpson and his mother for half an hour without ever looking at them directly enough to receive a gracious and condescending smile, she walked back up Myrtle Street and meditated on the misfortune of having been born without the ability to draw which was about to take Nellie Clark as far from the Piedmont Driving Club as the Rue Notre Dame des Champs in Paris, and without the ability to sing which was about to take Isabel Ambler as far from the Country Club of Virginia as the Piazza Aspromonte in Milan. She began to think that even if she had to do the dreadful thing called diminishing her principal, she might go away and cultivate her ability to have ideas, and that when the comfortable retirement of bereavement was almost over, she might postpone both a husband and reappearance in ball-rooms by looking at those capitals of Europe which she was most tired of hearing her acquaintances describe. And she began to consider the pleasant possibility that her boat was just as likely to sink as the Titanic had been, or that she might be able to get a fever in the Roman coliseum, although she knew that the water and the climate of Rome had improved since the timely death of Daisy Miller. For the first time, she knew how sorry she was that a satisfactory husband between eight and twelve is necessary to a woman's dignity. And for the first time, she suspected that the Virgin Mary and her son made a more charming picture because his father was in heaven, and she wondered just why there is nothing strange about being a wife and why there is something very strange about being a husband and a father, and just why men should love their children.

After the evening when Neal Lumpkin finally became damp around his near-sighted eyes and then began to breathe so noticeably that Katharine Faraday acquired a permanent distaste for breathing, she was never able to look at him again, and she was obliged to answer his telephone calls and his notes with a very polite note which told him that she was sure providence had not intended her for his wife. She considered telling him that she did not think providence had intended her for any one's wife, but she was afraid that even vanity might not always keep him from showing her note to some satisfactory young man whom she might possibly want to marry some day. She would also have liked to tell him that if she should ever be reduced to making her own living, she would rather make it by day than by night. And since she could not bring herself to write anything so unbecoming a southern lady in a letter, or even to say it to Sarah Rutledge or Nellie Clark, she bought a red notebook and saved her perishable phrase by entering it in the alphabetical place where she thought she would be most likely to find it at the distant date when she would be old enough and far enough from Atlanta to make conversational use of a remark which would not be really felicitous from any one except a richly dowered widow in a comedy of manners. She had begun to suspect that Atlanta was not likely to provide a satisfactory hero for the romance of Katharine Faraday, and even if Neal Lumpkin had not been obliged to breathe, she would still have felt that settling down to become the mother of Lumpkins was not the best use of a life spent in a world which contained Egyptologists and Italian princes and diplomats. And when she decided that she must go to New York and listen to academic lectures about the plays which were still called the modern drama, she realised that even if she did not hear any very interesting facts about John Millington Synge and Anton Chekhov, she might at least hear them from an interesting instructor—and from an instructor who might enjoy moulding a skeleton key to all knowledge for a girl whom she still found surprisingly pretty when she considered the destructive effect cleverness usually has on good looks. But she had no idea that she was looking for an actor who could carry on the rôle whose prologue had been elegantly played by Robert Carter and whose first act had been very badly played by Henry Brown. Even after she discovered that the lecturer was satisfactorily called Chauncey Brewster Howe, and that he was a doctor of philosophy from a German university of which she had never heard and which looked down its nose at Heidelberg—of which she had heard when she read a play about its students with the instructor at Mrs. Randolph's School whose early classes had increased her disapproval of people who liked coffee—she did not think of him as the third actor who had played the rôle of the hero in the romantic drama of Katharine Faraday and the scholarly gentleman. Before he had finished his satisfactorily horrified exposition of the religion and the married life exposed in a play called Ghosts, Katharine Faraday had asked him if he had any idea why fathers loved their children. She did not connect her question with his invitation to have dinner with him at a restaurant called Guffanti's, which she considered a pleasantly Mediterranean setting. But when he told her about his forefather who had assisted at the hanging of Major André and whose portrait was still in Independence Hall, she was sure his genealogical confidences must mean that he was pleased with the georgette iris on her new Crocker hat, although she did not suppose he knew they were on a Crocker hat. And she thought they probably meant that he shared the opinion of the young man who had already published a rondo and a sonnet in Life, and who proposed to try the critical faculties of any necessary number of editors with a triolet about a girl whose voice was like the falling petals of a magnolia blossom.

Katharine Faraday had never even considered reading a dialogue of Plato's, and she thought her Crocker hat and her magnolia voice, and her ability to ask questions which allowed long and learned answers, had moved Doctor Howe to something she thought was called Platonic friendship. She supposed that this classic emotion caused him to take her down to see interesting plays like Romance and interestingly titled and delicately veiled dancers like Lady Constance Stuart-Richardson. And she thought that an equally classic interest caused him to take her away from diversions he found inadequate to make her spirit more Greek or her temperament more Latin. She even thought that it caused him to give her a glass of beer and a goose liver sandwich to make her spirit more Teutonic and to justify the hour he occupied in expressing his opinions of the American periodicals which evidently did not know that a Lady Constance is always an Englishwoman who has not achieved a marriage as distinguished as her birth. She was not able to like the beer, but she was able to drink it more slowly than she had drunk rusty water at the Calhoun Street School, and to finish it just after Doctor Howe finished proving America's ignorance that a bishop is necessarily either a man of limited intelligence or a man who is holding his tongue and suffering for the youthful mistake of involving his beliefs with his livelihood. She was not much surprised by his apparent conviction that those ignorances and the absence of tables and chairs on the sidewalks were equally unfortunate, or by the pleasure he seemed to find in proving that he had been born in the most illiterate of all countries, and she did not have to act an interest in a learned narrative which was addressed exclusively to her. But she was able to sink down through his discourse long enough to decide that at last she could please a masculine audience and herself by talking about the minister who did not know why the Children of Israel settled on a golden calf, and about her recent discovery that she had always disliked major prophets, and about her belated discovery that none of the Bible's authors had a sense of humour—certainly not the author who was commonly supposed to have inspired all the others. When he told her that Jesus certainly had a delicate and Jesuitical wit, she was very much pleased with him and with herself, and she told him that he was the first man who had ever talked to her as if his mind and hers were not the relative sizes of their pocket-handkerchiefs. After a week of beer and goose liver and of Doctor Howe's conversation, she had a new birth as sudden and as exciting and as satisfactory as her sudden acquisition of balance on a bicycle had been. But instead of the new birth she had wept for when she was ten years old, it was a sudden pleasant conviction that she had been right about the First Presbyterian Church and the First Presbyterian Church's Sunday School, and that her mother and her father and the minister and Elsie Dinsmore and Saint Paul had all been wrong. She thought that she felt exactly as relieved as she had felt on the afternoon when she was going down in an elevator after she had her first wisdom-tooth out, and that she would never again have to think about a god who admired flesh and blood sacrifices so much that he had felt obliged to make himself a son of flesh and blood and then to drive three large nails in the son before he could let her off from the blazing hell he had felt obliged to make long before—doubtless with an imperative wave of his right hand and with one objective noun and one imperative verb. But since Doctor Howe chose the same evening for showing her an undeniably English book in which an Oxford lecturer had mentioned the name of C. B. Howe respectfully enough to disagree with his views concerning the Antigone of Aeschylus and the Antigone of Sophocles, she was so much taken up with being interesting to such an important scholar that she did not think very long about the relief of a future which would not be spent in a fiery hell—not nearly as long as she had thought about the painless loss of her wisdom-tooth.

After a month of Doctor Howe's official and unofficial instructions, Katharine Faraday had learned that aspiring club members are mistaken when they think Ibsen and Shaw and Chekhov and the eighteenth Lord Dunsany can be understood by people who are contentedly ignorant of Aristotle and Julius Caesar Scaliger and Euripides and Ben Jonson. She had learned how man came by the curious idea that he had something called a soul and how he came by the idea that all his redeemers must be the offspring of comparatively unassisted virgins, she had learned that in spite of being a woman Sappho was the greatest of all lyric poets and that coincidences in fiction are not legitimate, and she had learned the names and the achievements of the most important European restaurants, and the names of a good many liqueurs besides benedictine and of a good many cigarettes besides Pall Malls. But she was more interested in her discovery that the pleasantest feminine situation is a restaurant chair across a small table from a man who is not too much more taken with her than she is with him, and who is not noticeably less taken with her. She was also more interested in her discovery that something was beginning to go wrong with the evenings she and Doctor Howe spent together. Her summer with Henry Brown had prepared her for her summer with Doctor Howe by teaching her to ask satisfactory questions, and by teaching her that sitting opposite an unmarried man is a much more enviable situation than sitting opposite a man who has damaged his social value by being legally married. But it had not taught her to avoid the mistake she had made when she sat down at Doctor Howe's feet on the first morning of their acquaintance, and neither had it taught her how to get up and sit down by his side, or to suspect that he did not know how to go about raising her to his side so that he could raise her to his knee. She supposed the difficulty must be that his genealogical distinctions were all based on the incomprehensible aristocracy of ancestors who had come to America on a little boat called the Mayflower. And since she did not know how to penetrate the calmness of such an inheritance, she decided that she must take away the charms she was sure he had the ability to appreciate, and that she must increase her importance in his eyes by going to the countries in which he would have liked to be himself.

When Katharine Faraday sailed economically away from New York on an Italian boat called the America, she was interested in the remarkable although foreseen coincidence that she was leaving the new world on a boat which was named for it and which was manned by the compatriots of its discoverer, and that she was leaving it under the sign of Libra which was shining down when Christopher Columbus damaged the health and the literature of the Caucasian race by setting European feet on it. But she was a good deal more interested in her three baskets of Page and Shaw's chocolates and her box of Maillard's marrons glacés, her box of crimson roses and her box of orchids and her box of violets inset with two gardenias, in her copy of a red book called Youth's Encounter, in her three little address books bound in a shade of purple enough like a prayer-book to recognise her presumably diminishing sorrow, in the twenty-seven letters of which four were from comparatively marriageable young men and in the three telegrams of which one was from a completely marriageable young man, and in the valcdictory presence of Doctor Chauncey Brewster Howe and the seventy-ninth and eightieth of the literary papers which he had published and which he had brought for her instructive amusement during her seven Atlantic days and her three Mediterranean days. And she was still more interested in the long split in the left side of her narrow black skirt and in the curve of the white organdie collar which flared up against the parted point of black hair at the back of her neck, and in the little black hat with the crown like half an egg and the inch of brim which moved Doctor Howe to the quotation of Richard Lovelace and Sir Charles Sedley. She did not enjoy hearing rhymes and iambics just as she was embarking, but she knew that the quotation of cavalier poetry implied a romantic interest, and since the presence of Isabel Ambler and Isabel Ambler's aunt would keep her from discovering the effect of her experiment, she was drawn far enough up from her sedentary position at his feet to try the effect of smiling up into his large blue eyes. When she was suffering from the impressive decisiveness of a departing boat, she had no idea that she was drawing down a premature curtain on the romantic drama of Katharine Faraday and the scholarly gentleman. She thought that she would lie all day and all night in the seclusion of her upper berth with her cheek against the name which she thought was a distinguished name, and which Doctor Howe had written on his seventy-ninth and eightieth literary papers, and that she would feel her fountain rising and falling and dropping its electric spray down her body and that for eight months she would not think of anything except the June day when she would sail back into New York harbor and see Doctor Howe waiting miraculously for her on the pier. She was sure she had made a mistake in going away even to the places where he would have liked to be, and her only consolation was the foresight which had warned her that she would feel mortifyingly lonely on too moonlit an ocean, and which had made her persuade Isabel Ambler's aunt to change her sailing date by inventing a superstition that settled the sailing dates of a great many well-bred southern ladies and gentlemen for a great many years—a superstition about the perils of crossing an ocean except during the dark of the moon, when good luck pursues potatoes and all the other fruits of the earth which find their fulfillment in it, and which Katharine Faraday said could only mean that people who rashly cross an ocean under a full moon are very likely to rise dripping from the sea on the day of judgment instead of rising more tidily from Hollywood Cemetery or from West View Cemetery.

When Katharine Faraday drove from Sorrento to Amalfi, she suffered from her recent parting with the tall young compatriot of Christopher Columbus who had helped her to endure the beauty of phosphorus lit spray in the Mediterranean, and she suffered from the mortification of driving above such a moonlit bay with no more romantic companions than Isabel Ambler and Isabel Ambler's aunt. When she looked at the dark blue bay of Salerno between the coral columns of Poseidon's temple at Paestum, she suffered from the mortification of looking at it with an aging lady who had come to Italy because Richmond recognised travel as a decorous reason for leaving off a crape veil and for emerging from a back parlour, and she suffered still more from looking across the marble and the lizards at a girl in a brown checked coat and skirt who was turning her straight young back on the blue bay to embrace a tall young man with whom she had almost certainly walked down a church aisle less than a month before. When she looked at the House of the Faun in Pompeii, she suffered from the presence of the same happy bride in a grey squirrel coat, and when she went to a crimson-brocaded room to kiss the Holy Father's ring, she could not enjoy her emotions because of the same happy bride's presence in a white coat and skirt and a white lace mantilla. She had been sure she would feel a magnificent sense of achievement when she walked out of an ordinary grey-cushioned compartment and heard the rising and falling fountains of Rome, but after she had missed a train in Naples and suffered four hours of an Italian wedding party and two hours of a priest who opened a folded newspaper and took out the garments which suddenly transformed him into a Dominican monk as alarmingly black and white as Savonarola, she told Isabel Ambler that she had suffered too much to be surprised by finding herself before the baths of Diocletian, and that she would not have been surprised if she had found herself before the throne of God. When she looked at the Pantheon, she would have liked to tell Isabel Ambler's aunt that if all the contented members of Saint Paul's parish in Richmond and Saint Michael's parish in Charleston were chained before it for three days, they might possibly be brought to realise how a church looks when it is really old. When she dined at the American embassy, she forgot to use the knife which should have helped her fork out with the fish, and she was never able to talk about her first evening in a palace with much satisfaction, but when she walked under an arch of the coliseum, she heard a lion roar so plainly that the afternoon remained permanently in her repertoire as an illustration of her sensitive nature. When she walked into the Accademia delle Belli Arte, she was very much interested in the difference between the minute before she looked through a door and saw Botticelli's Spring and the minute after, and she considered it a more important difference than the difference between the minute when Edward Cabot had been in the room with her and the minute after he had gone out. When she drove from Florence to Siena, she enjoyed seeing the house of Santa Caterina because they shared a Christian name. When she stepped into a gondola with only Isabel Ambler and Isabel Ambler's aunt, she was mortifyingly lonely even with the left side of her blouse sheltering the letter from Doctor Howe which she had paid two lire to read in a hot bath the night before, and with her little black bag sheltering the letter from Christopher Columbus's tall young compatriot which she had paid two lire to read in a hot bath three nights before. She was not consoled by her own cleverness when she thought of writing a poem about how Venice woke early on an April morning and saw her own loveliness smiling up at her from her own canals, and how Venice gazed on her own loveliness until she became a Narcissus among nations. Even after she had entered her only poetical inspiration in her red notebook, she felt obliged to smile across a narrow canal at a young man who looked like a young gentleman and who was singing to his guitar. He dropped his guitar and answered her smile by a deliberate exposition of the mysteries George Faraday had already revealed to her accidentally, and after she had become able to read books which mentioned the United States Military Academy and the United States Artillery Corps, she was still unable to read a book which mentioned Venice. When she wept before The Last Supper in Milan, she was so much pleased with such a proof of her emotional nature that she conceived an admiration for Leonardo da Vinci which lasted all her life. When she went to see a tragedy called Phèdre at the Comédie Française, she thought that the acting and the scenery were very much like the acting and the scenery in the play called Uncle Tom's Cabin which she and Isabel Ambler and Margaret Cameron had slipped away from Mrs. Randolph's School to see, and she thought that the Frenchman on the strapontin beside her breathed like Neal Lumpkin on the evening when he had become damp around the eyes. When she bought an unbecoming hat and the milliner refused to change it for a becoming hat, she twisted the hat up before his greedy eyes, and she conceived a distaste for the French character which survived the acquisition of two surprisingly becoming violet hats and two surprisingly becoming violet frocks and one surprisingly becoming violet and fuchsia evening frock—which she considered a pleasant symbol for the day on which she would end her public regret for Arthur

Faraday—and a sufficiently becoming mauve tweed coat and skirt, and which survived the battles of the Marne and even the siege of Verdun. When she looked at the fountains of Versailles, she looked at them in the society of a young man who was called Murray Whiting and who had been born in Mobile and she suffered the same hot untidy feeling she had suffered when she went to tea at the New Willard with two compatriots who had not been properly introduced to her, but she felt obliged to suffer it, because she could not go to the Bal Tabarin without a young man and she could not go back to Atlanta and admit that she had not danced in the hall which she thought was the wickedest place in Paris. When she looked at Napoleon's bath-room in the Palace of Fontainebleau, she decided that no really rational man would have thought such an ugly and uncomfortable bath-room sufficient reward for supervising battles in countries where the weather is as conspicuous as it is in Egypt and Russia. When she read the inscription on Oscar Wilde's tomb after she had laid six black iris on it, she went at once to look at the Hotel d'Alsace, and she distressed Isabel Ambler's aunt by wanting to spend a night in the room where he died so that she could preserve the emotions of the night in some form of literature. When she went to the little chapel of Saint Hubert at Amboise above the Loire, she took a small sheaf of leaves which she thought were laurel leaves, and she laid them on the stones under which she thought the bones of Leonardo da Vinci were reposing. When she walked down the Haymarket, she pleased the Virginian pride of Isabel Ambler's aunt by pointing out the strange resemblance between the most plebeian English features and the most aristocratic Charlestonian features, and when she went to Oxford, she was distressed because the porter of Magdalen College was unable to point out the room in which Compton Mackenzie had eaten the bread and cheese of his first lunch as a member of the college. And when she went to Cork, she drove out to Blarney Castle and risked her life in giving its most celebrated stone a kiss which she thought might make her conversation interesting even to the younger members of the Piedmont Driving Club.

When Katharine Faraday looked up from the low little boat which had brought her and Isabel Ambler's aunt and some hundreds of their actual and future compatriots out from Queenstown to meet the condescending pause of the tall White Star liner Oceanic, she met the waiting eyes of Murray Whiting. She knew that she had no idea why men did the extraordinary things they all seemed to do under the same conditions, but she thought his deliberate presence on her boat suggested that his interest in her was at least as ardent as it was honourable. She was afraid that if she went on looking up she might not be sufficiently protected by the presence of Isabel Ambler's aunt or even by the publicity of a deck filled with collectors of Irish lace and blackthorn sticks and little tin pots of shamrock, and she walked up the gangway with her eyes fixed regretfully on the long white cathedral of Saint Columba. By the time the white cathedral had been overpowered by the greenness which she told Murray Whiting was the only European scene that had not disappointed her since they had looked down together at the fountains of Versailles, she had listened to the recital of everything he had eaten during his first day in London. Before he had begun describing the virtues of the bacon with which he had begun his second day at Berner's Hotel, she had begun to think that if the public admiration of unpresentable men did not seem to draw presentable men as successfully as china eggs draw edible eggs, she would not have been able to endure either his conversation or the mortification of being publicly admired by a man with such a retiring lower lip and such a plaid cap and such a blue tie and such conversation. Before the satisfactory greenness of Ireland had been overpowered by the dull imprisoning greenness of the Atlantic Ocean, she had opened her red notebook at a page she considered appropriate, and she had entered a conviction that when a bride walks down the aisle of a church with a man whom she has just publicly endorsed at its altar, she is risking a whole congregation of comparisons with Titania, Queen of the Fairies. And although she would not have elaborated such an unladylike idea even in a notebook, she began to wonder if a Russian coronet and a brocaded satin train lined with silver and a sheaf of calla lilies would entirely prevent the mortification she might reasonably feel during a public announcement that she had found a man with whom she would be willing to share a bed and a son. But before she had found an opportunity of retiring into The Last Days of Pompeii, pride had triumphed over jealous caution, and he had interrupted a report of his inquiries into the reason for the greenness of the cabbage he had refused on the evening of his fourth day in London, and he had told her that he was sharing a cabin with a young Austrian baron called Lothar Falkenhayn, and he had also told her that Baron Lothar Falkenhayn was going from his own diplomatic post in Rome to stay with one of his colleagues in Washington. Katharine Faraday was able not to express any greater interest in Murray Whiting's noble cabin companion than she had expressed in undesirably green cabbage, but she went down to her own cabin and took a great deal of trouble to achieve a beautiful roundness for the two coils of black hair which covered her ears. And in spite of the cautions Isabel Ambler's aunt gave her against beginning an acquaintance in a frock she could not possibly surpass during the seven evenings of the voyage, her returning belief in love at first sight would not allow her to go up to dinner in anything except the violet and fuchsia frock she had not meant to wear until October.

When Katharine Faraday sat down beside Baron Lothar Falkenhayn, she realised that at last she was sitting beside a man who belonged to the great world, and she realized that before he drank his coffee she must prove to him how much cleverer she was than most girls who were as good looking as she thought she was in her violet and fuchsia frock. While she was doing her hair, she had thought about the precisely appropriate use of the two rules for important conversations she had entered in her red notebook on the evening after she had lunched at Frascati with the third secretary of the American embassy in Rome. The first rule forbade her to ask a question unless she was sure she was asking it of a man who would enjoy answering it, and as soon as she looked at Baron Lothar Falkenhayn and his dinner coat and his bottle of Reschiglian, she was sure he would enjoy being asked if Arthur Schnitzler had painted a portrait of Viennese life when he described the earlier affairs of Anatol. Her question was so successful that she did not have to worry about the application of the rule which forbade her to make a remark merely for the pleasure she found in saying something aloud, and which did not allow her to use either the best or the freshest examples of her repertoire unless she was sure that she was saying them for a man who would enjoy hearing them. It was even so successful that when she walked out to her deck-chair the next morning, she found Baron Lothar Falkenhayn's chair beside it, and Baron Lothar Falkenhayn sitting in his chair and wearing a top coat which seemed to be grey, but which a tangent chair and the July sun revealed as a coat subtly woven of a thousand subtle shades, and which convinced her that she was probably beginning the second scene in the first act of a play which might be the high comedy of Katharine Faraday and the young Viennese diplomat. Baron Lothar Falkenhayn began the scene with his attentions to her new heliotrope rug and his inquiries after her health and her breakfast and his compliments on her coiffure, and he carried it on almost as satisfactorily with the history of the June day when he had ascended Mount Aetna while it was interestingly active. He followed the history of the day when he conquered the mountain with his approval of a Parisian dancer called Gaby, who was so celebrated that his compatriots and Katharine Faraday's were willing to put down five hundred francs for the pleasure of going back to their own countries and boasting about the evening when they had taken her to dine in the Bois de Boulogne, and who was so amiable that she always threw in her society until the next morning. And he followed his approval of the celebrated Gaby with an authentic version of Crown Prince Rudolf's death and of the consolations the Emperor Franz Josef had found for his old age. Katharine Faraday remembered that the heroes of Schnitzler's comedies usually offer the heroines an affection which is a good deal more ardent than it is honourable, and she began to wonder if Baron Lothar Falkenhayn would have told the same histories to a young lady whose coat of arms also had enough quarterings to admit her to the throne room of the Hofburg, or if he thought that American virgins of twenty-two were in the habit of being audiences for such anecdotes. Since she had no idea whether or not she should have felt that her youthful innocence had been insulted, she did not retire to the protection of Isabel Ambler's aunt, or to the further revelation that Lord Lytton's prose could hardly have been duller if he had been born in Massachusetts. But she satisfied propriety and the calming of one jealousy and the stimulating of another jealousy by smiling an invitation to Murray Whiting when he walked down the deck with the six-year-old twins in whom he had just begun to show a great interest, and she did not say either to him or to Baron Lothar Falkenhayn that she thought a taste for children and dogs showed an inability to produce conversation which was satisfactory to men and women. She also began to risk seasickness by staying in her cabin most of the morning, and before she had finished reading The Last Days of Pompeii, her confidence in the great Victorians had vanished with her confidence in a future life and in rhyming iambics, and she was beginning to wonder if she had been right when she abandoned her novel because it would necessarily have been an American novel. On the evening when he told her a story about an innocent friend of his who had found himself engaged to an American girl without a fortune, and who had been obliged to ask her family why she should become royal and imperial ambassadress to Mexico without giving anything in return for such a position, she began to wonder how mothers set about bringing up a daughter when they do not know whether they are bringing her up to be a duchess or a stenographer. She began to feel even sorrier that she had not been born in a country where parents can admit the necessity of providing their daughters with husbands, and she began to wonder if a literary reputation would provide her with the equivalent of a fortune even if it did not provide her with a fortune. She was afraid that he had told her the story as a polite way of assuring her that he was less innocent than his friend, and even after he had told her that only a very remarkable American woman could interest a European man for five days, she could not endure the idea of having him suspect her of wanting to marry him, and she told him that she was expecting her fiancé to meet her at the pier in New York. She still lay in her berth and felt her fountain rise and fall when she planned the possibility of finding herself drifting down the Atlantic Ocean with Lothar Falkenhayn in the lifeboat on whose canvas cover she had sat beside him the night before, and she still dreaded the approaching shore of America. And she was delighted when she heard that the heir to the Austrian throne had been shot, because she liked the idea of hearing that an Austrian archduke had died while she was sitting beside an Austrian attaché with whom she did not doubt she was very much in love. On the night before she would be obliged to leave Baron Lothar Falkenhayn with a smile and to meet Doctor Howe with a smile unless there should be a saving wreck before morning, she sat beside him on the lifeboat and he held her hand under her heliotrope rug, and she suffered almost as satisfactorily as she would have suffered if she had been leaving a man who loved her tenderly, and leaving him for an aging scholar to whom she was bound by her honour.

Katharine Faraday was always able to enjoy saying that she had lost all confidence in her own intelligence on the day when a war followed the assassination she had enjoyed so much, and she was able to enjoy feeling that she was completely different from all the American women who enjoyed the war so much even after it ceased to be a merely European war. She thought that her reason was entirely responsible for her convictions, and when she enjoyed feeling broad-minded because she did not believe that all the little boys in Belgium had been deprived of their right hands or that all the women in Belgium had been found raving and naked and breastless and virtueless in abandoned German trenches, she knew that she was remembering the night when Lothar Falkenhayn had held her hand until morning without offering her the indignity of a kiss, and she knew that she was also remembering the Frenchman who had breathed on the strapontin beside her and the

Frenchman from whom she had bought the unbecoming hat. She enjoyed making conversational use of the words Doctor Howe had taught her, and after she had observed the clergymen who enjoyed believing that French cats and English officers were crucified side by side on barn doors, she enjoyed saying that Christianity is a sadist's religion, and after patriotism introduced large American flags of the best quality into churches, she enjoyed saying that the American clergy were reducing their own god to a tribal deity. She liked to say that she could not possibly go to dances while Doctor Howe was in danger, and she wrote long letters to him on her father's large paper and then copied them on slightly smaller sheets of lavender paper imported from a little shop under the arches of the Théâtre National de l'Odéon. She knew that uniforms had been painful to her long after she was sure she could never have been really in love with a man whose conversation showed so little erudition as Edward Cabot's, and even after the coast artillery had given up crimson stripes on their trousers and crimson linings in their capes. But she liked to say that the mere sight of Camp

Gordon lowered her vitality, and that she had caught a cold on every one of the three afternoons when the exigent position of guest in a motor car had obliged her to see the horrors of compulsory existence in barracks. She also liked to say that those three afternoons made her give ten dollars to the American Red Cross and that they made her buy two of the bonds which were called liberty bonds, but she gave the ten dollars and bought the two bonds because she did not admire martyrs, and because she was too well-bred to do anything so inelegant and so uncomfortable as going to prison for her opinions. She always said that she did not like to knit because so many concerts were ruined for her by the sight of a hundred thumbs disobeying the composer's rhythm, and that she did not enjoy a society given over to socks and sweaters any more than she enjoyed herself in Asheville, where society was based on participation in the same physical exercises. But before she had quite begun to say that a woman who hopes to enjoy life must turn her back on life and pay no attention to it, the war provided her with the advantage of talking to the first English writer who had ever sat down to lunch beside her just after she had heard him give a lecture. Since his lecture and her researches had proved that he would enjoy answering her question, she asked him to tell her just how the members of its colleges acquired such incomparable education at Oxford, and she did not interrupt his answer except to explain that the small fowls were chickens sacrificed in their early youth and that the rolls were hot because they were meant to be split horizontally and filled with butter. None of her fellow guests could doubt that she had eclipsed a bishop and a governor, and she told all her acquaintances that in spite of his sixty years, the Honourable Charles Murray had every mental and physical and social and spiritual grace. But she did not tell them that she had seen thirty women standing around him on the little platform in Egleston Hall, and that she had observed their struggles to find one sentence which would make him realise how superior their admiration was to the admiration of all other women. And she did not tell them when she decided that even the handicap of being born an American, and even the horror of printing American sentences which her signature would endorse as mortifyingly as marriage would endorse a man, should no longer keep from proving her cleverness in print, and proving it once for all time and all men,

Even after Katharine Faraday began to consider the possibility of becoming important herself instead of waiting to find honourable favour in the sight of a man so celebrated that he could make her important merely by allowing her to use his names with a suitably apologetic prefix, she still thought a presentable man between eight o'clock and twelve was as necessary as a violet velvet evening coat and nicely waved hair. She was still unable to enjoy an opera called The Love of the Three Kings unless she was sitting beside a presentable man who was more interested in her profile than he was in the beautiful death of Lucrezia Bori, and she was still unable to enjoy the third Leonora overture unless she was sitting beside a man who would have been likely to name his overtures for her if he had been able to write overtures. And even in a taffeta frock which changed from violet to gold and which flared fashionably just below her waist, she was unable to sit between two women and weep at a play called Justice when an already widowed contemporary was sitting in front of her between two men. She sat down every morning and tried to think with a purple pencil in her right hand, but her admirers continued to succeed each other like the courses of a state dinner. And since the days between evenings and afternoons with her prevalent admirer were always filled by hours spent in reading about the things he was interested in, she acquired a great deal of information about coffer-dams and orange-peel buckets before she lost all interest in engineering after she had suffered the mortification of public suspicion that she was willing to be admired by an engineer who had let the same man pay for his dinner twice in succession. She became convinced that her mother was right about the extreme unlikeliness of finding a presentable man who had been born in Connecticut, and she decided that she was in love with a tall young surgeon who had been born in one of the less undesirable towns in Alabama. She began to dislike all trained nurses as much as her mammy did, and to share her doubt about the impregnability of their virtue, and she began to read about sarcoma and thyroid glands and surgical technique and to discover that newspapers were evidently wrong when they politely ascribed all operations to appendicitis. When her tall young surgeon was suspected of an operation which was not for appendicitis, she did not decide that she had never been in love with him. But she wrote in her notebook that every time she saw a girl shopping with a baby held hotly in her arms, she decided again to be good and to let any one else who liked be clever, and she also wrote that she did not like the idea of becoming an impoverished spinster, but that she liked it better than she liked the idea of domesticated poverty. She decided that she had fallen in love with a young journalist who had been born in Nashville, and she had read about Delane of the Times and about Joseph Pulitzer and Charles Dana before he was distracted from her by a girl who had red hair and whom she suspected of having a great deal of money. She decided that she had fallen in love with a man who already had a satisfactory wife, and she had begun to share his admiration for a book called The Interpretation of Dreams and for another book called Sons and Lovers before she saw him for the last time at the picnic to which he forgot to bring a pocket-handkerchief. She decided that she was in love with a man whose elegant walk would have made him as impressive in Hyde Park as he was when he stepped down from the portals of Saint Bartholomew's Church into Park Avenue, and she had read three volumes of the Duc de Saint Simon's memoirs and one volume of the Marquise de Sévigné's letters and two volumes of the very small type of Charles Greville's journal and all of Queen Victoria's Highland diary before he told her that he was about to be married to a widow who had a box at the Metropolitan Opera House on odd Mondays. She began to believe that any one who thinks badly of any man long enough is sure to find himself justified, and she was never able to think that she was in love with any man who lived in the same town with her, but every night she lay awake for hours planning letters which she could not have written if she had not been able to believe that they would be the letters which would be eagerly opened first or tenderly opened last.

When she had occupied four years with writing and rewriting letters on sheets of her father's large paper and then carefully copying them on her own slightly smaller sheets of lavender paper, Katharine Faraday thought that she had finally learned to write a letter which would seem sufficiently ardent when its purple-lined envelope was torn open, and not ardent at all if it were read again just as it was about to be burned. And she thought that her most valuable textbook had been a blue book called A Musical Motley, which she had read during the months when admiration for a pianist called Josef Hofmann left her unable to read anything except lives of Chopin and George Sand and Liszt and Hummel and John Field and Robert and Clara Schumann and Wagner and his Isolde, and which taught her to write love-letters by instructing a young musical critic in the most ingenious methods of satisfying a difficult taste and simultaneously avoiding successful libel suits. She had just begun to remember with satisfaction that Pallas Athena and Jane Austen and Agnes Repplier were all spinsters. And after she had eaten broiled chicken and asparagus aspic beside the Honourable Charles Murray, she had been able to keep her mind off her letters to Dick Crawford long enough to write eight pages which she thought composed an essay because she thought their style was more important than their subject, and which she thought nevertheless managed to prove that marriage has a bad effect on a woman's writing, and that George Eliot and George Sand might easily have been writing to prove that living in sin is just as injurious to feminine literary style as a union preceded by a civil and a religious ceremony. She did not see why Virginal Succession should not prove her cleverness to the world once for all, and although she could not hope that the celebrated Charles Carrington would like it, she did not see why it should not prove her cleverness to a writer called Frederick Thomas. She thought that he had a great deal more reputation than either his style or his information should have allowed him, and she was so annoyed by his increasing celebrity that she wanted him to fall in love with her. She had carefully calculated every sentence in it for him, but she was not sure that either Frederick Thomas or the rest of the literary world would be able to appreciate her peculiarly subtle cleverness, and she thought that only the comparative absence of publicity would make sending her essay off to an unappreciative periodical any less painful than standing in a school yard and waiting for a tap which would allow her to play Prisoner's Base or standing in a ballroom and waiting for a partner who would make her eligible to dance. Even after the Honourable Charles Murray had spoken her name among the pleasures of his American tour, and spoken it in the public prints, she was not able to make herself do anything more useful than reading Virginal Succession again with complete satisfaction. But when she went to a lunch where she sat beside the plump young mother who had once been the little girl whose carefully curled hair and aquiline nose and pleated crimson crêpe de chine frock had been a divine commission to rule the red clay yard of the Calhoun Street School, she found that the little girl had not become anything more enviable than a president of the North Carolina Federation of Women's Clubs. And before she had eaten her bird and her wild rice, she had decided that Isabel Ambler had certainly been married long enough not to be annoyingly fond of her husband, and that she would go up again to stay with her in Baltimore, and that she would have herself seated at lunch beside a young woman called Virginia Wise, who had given up spending her money on increasing her beauty, and who was now spending a good deal of it on a yellow magazine called Egg-Nog, which was proving her own cleverness to her own world, and which was obliged to surround her casual sentences and her exclamation points with the verses a few other southern ladies composed during sermons, and the little sketches some other southern ladies enjoyed making from their conversations with their cooks.

Before she sat down beside Virginia Wise on the sofa which had survived the evening when Isabel Ambler's great-grandmother had refused the hand of George Washington, Katharine Faraday had decided that only complete confidence in the world's ability to appreciate her charms would have allowed Virginia Wise to think she could look more important than the high-crowned yellow hat she was wearing. When she invited Virginal Succession into the November number she would be bringing out in December, Katharine Faraday was sure she must be completely confident that her world would consider the little story called The Onyx What-Not, with which she would triumphantly follow her own yellow title-page, a better proof of the beneficial literary effect of celibacy than all the Jane Austens and Elizabeth Brownings in Katharine Faraday's eight pages. When she took her newest contributor out to share a stool at Charles Carrington's feet, Katharine Faraday was sure she would not have been invited into the celebrated orange-lined motor, or tucked under its sable rug, if Viriginia Wise had not been serenely confident that Charles Carrington would find her own conversation and her own orange hair and her own wide brown velvet hat more charming than Katharine Faraday's conversation and her fuchsia hat and her black hair which had never enjoyed even the attention of a permanent wave. Katharine Faraday thought that Virginia Wise's hair and her eyes and her profile owed too much to Europe, and that her literary style owed too little, and since she knew that Charles Carrington apparently wrote from undraped models, she did not expect him to observe either the hats or the frocks at his feet. She was sure she would not be able to remember anything she wanted to be able to say she had said to him, and when she was not trying to memorize the little list of questions she thought he would enjoy answering—and which she thought would make him realise how superior her admiration was to Virginia Wise's admiration—she was wishing that Charles Carrington had already been enshrined among the forefathers who were too eminent for him to feel that he had added any distinction to his name by becoming the author of his eight novels, and that she was about to lay a green laurel wreath on his marble tomb instead of drinking his tea. When she was driving back through the Green Spring Valley, she had given up wishing that Charles Carrington was safely in a tomb where he could not refuse to accept her homage, and she was able to tell Virginia Wise that she would be willing to have a toothache for a week if she could have known for one minute what he was thinking while he was talking like a southern gentleman providing jasmine tea and hot anchovy sandwiches for two southern ladies. She was able to say that the idea of a man and a perambulator was only the ultimate proof of the absurdity of fatherhood, and that Charles Carrington's refusal to take any wife had added the only distinction which could possibly have been added to his profile and his forefathers and his Georgian house of the third period and his eight books, and that any woman who wanted to walk down a church aisle with him ought to realise the social and literary crime she would be committing if she decreased his distinction as definitely as she had decreased her motor car's value when she drove it across a sidewalk. When she slipped off her black velvet frock and looked into Isabel Ambler's mirror at the new white crêpe de chine chemise which was one of the lustral rites with which she had prepared herself to sit at Charles Carrington's feet, she saw that it was curiously streaked with green and scarlet stripes. But she did not think the rising and falling of her fountain was caused by the emotion she called love, and since she did not often think about the religion she had enjoyed losing, she did not suspect that she might be feeling something like the emotion a young novice might feel for Jesus Christ. And she did not suspect that Charles Carrington's refusal of the married state made him more interesting to her in almost exactly the same way Jesus Christ's refusal of it made him more interesting to virgins who had a taste for tinkering with their souls instead of a taste for tinkering with a literary style. But she knew she would not have found Charles Carrington's continued existence so satisfactory if he had not talked to her about their common sufferings in the pursuit of a style, and she was sure she would never again be conscious of a man's existence unless he enjoyed the distinction of being a celebrated writer—not any more than she would ever again walk into a shop and see the hats which did not enjoy the distinction of belonging to the violet side of the millinery rainbow.

When she went back to stay with Virginia Wise in April, Katharine Faraday was already more distressed by seeing the belated November number of Egg-Nog than she had ever been by seeing books which mentioned the United States Artillery Corps or by books which mentioned the canals of Venice. She was suffering from the mortification of having endorsed such American sentences by signing them with her name, and only her respect for celebrity and the admirable draping of her new fuchsia georgette evening gown—which celebrity's approval of her American sentences made her feel important enough to wear—gave her the courage to sit down at the same dinner table with Charles Carrington and Frederick Thomas and Max Boeckmann. But before she had finished one Bacardi cocktail, she had begun to realise again the advantage of talking to a man whose tastes and distastes were recorded in the public prints. She had managed to slip two quotations from Frederick

Thomas's sixth book into the middle of two of her own sentences, and she had been rewarded by a blue-eyed smile which surprised her from a man whose writing had led her to suppose that he looked like a bearded admiral called von Tirpitz. And since she had already discovered that a southern lady's charms are estimated entirely by their agreement with tradition and that her intelligence is judged entirely by her ability to disagree with tradition, she told him that she thought there was a great deal to be said for the Old South, but not nearly as much as people had already said. And she told him that she had recently begun to wonder what General Robert Edward Lee could really have been like, and just what his human weaknesses could possibly have been if he had any, and just what she had decided they were after she read a hundred or two of his letters, and then she said she could not imagine Beethoven with a rosary in his hands. She mentioned an Austrian doctor called Krafft-Ebing to show him that she did not expect to be answered in language suited to a southern lady, and she asked him just why fatherhood is so absurd and just why fathers love their children. She was sure he would enjoy telling her about the egotism which he considered the true reason, and he enjoyed his own views so much that he followed them with a long discussion of the reasons why no New Englander ever had been a gentleman and why no New Englander ever would be a gentleman—a discussion she was sure must be either a rehearsal for something he was about to write or a recital of something he had just written. She did not have to act an interest in a monologue which such an eminent author addressed exclusively to her, and before she had reached the climax of her artichoke she was sure that she was in love with the celebrated Frederick Thomas. When she went to lunch with him the next day, she was pleased that he held her hand tenderly after he had two glasses of white wine, but she was more pleased that a restaurant satisfactorily full of people saw her lunching with an author who had penetrated American literature as a banana penetrates a box of sandwiches. She would have been disappointed if he had not kissed her while he was driving her back to Virginia Wise's lemon yellow house, and if he had not told her that her literary style would be greatly improved by the loss of her virginity and that Pallas Athena's interest in Odysseus was at least maternal. When he asked her to go back to New York with him, she was surprised that she could not act an indignation she did not feel, and that her first offer of an affection which was at least as dishonourable as it was ardent did not make her feel anything except the awkwardness of saying she did not think she would enjoy being seduced. She was also surprised when she could not definitely refuse the honour of becoming mistress to a prince of prose, and when she only told him that she did not expect to be anything more than an episode to any man, but that she did not like the idea of being an incident even to him, and when she went on to tell that she seemed to be hopelessly virginal by nature and that whenever she saw a girl shopping with a baby held hotly in her arms, she decided again to be good and to let any one who liked be clever. She did not tell him that she was suffering the same hot untidy feeling she had suffered when she looked at the fountains of Versailles and the dancers at the Bal Tabarin in the illegitimate society of Murray Whiting. And she did not go to New York, but when she was back in Atlanta she thought she was sorry that she had not gone, and she lay in her nineteenth-century bed and dreamed dreams which she thought were giving her an insight into a nature very unlike the nature a southern lady should have had. She waited twice every day for the postman who would leave her whole body burning from the blazing fall of disappointment or who would leave it an alabaster lamp for the rise and fall of its electric spray. And even though they were nearly always written on a typewriter, and even though their capital letters always jumped up above their fellow members of the words which seemed to be scored for drums, she lay in her bed with her left hand against the envelope under her pillow, and sometimes she wept for five minutes because Frederick Thomas had wanted to get on to the third act while she wanted to linger in the second half of the first act. When she discovered that he had also been born under the sign of Virgo, she saluted his birthday with a chastely framed copy of the Saint Ursula whom Carpaccio painted lying coolly and virginally in her high wide bed. She gave up drinking cocktails because she did not like to suffer from a strange aching under what she still called her stomach, and she considered telling him that if she wanted a son she would like to share a son with him, and that she did not see why they should not produce something more admirable than the celebrated offspring of two celebrated English novelists. She never told him just that, but she went on suffering from her belief that she was in love with him until the day when she had her first letter from David Hofmann. On that day, an acquaintance with the theories of Sigmund Freud convinced her that she could not possibly be in love with Frederick Thomas, since she forgot to mail the letter she had written six times on her father's large sheets of paper, and then copied four times on her own lavender paper from the portico of the Théâtre National de l'Odéon.

Before she heard David Hofmann's voice and decided that she could say it was like a double-stopped violin, and then decided that she was certainly in love with him and that she had never been in love before, the second act of the cynical comedy of Katharine Faraday and the eminent author was played by a celebrated dramatist who was called Samuel King, but whose name was commonly supposed to resemble his father's only in being a less imperial translation into the English language, and whose celebrated profile was commonly supposed to include a somewhat more than Roman nose. When she sat down beside him on the golden satin chesterfield which faced the golden satin chesterfield on which Virginia Wise seemed to be giving Max Boeckmann the feeling that she was sitting at his feet and by his side and on his knee at the same time, Katharine Faraday was sure she could not provide the heroine with lines which would equal the lines a hero who was also a dramatist could provide for himself. But she managed to slip a quotation from his fifth play into the sentences in which she told him that she hoped he would not mind having her say how shockingly he was libelled by his photographs—photographs which made him look like a bookmaker who had enjoyed a good season. He replied with a discussion of the relation between an author's wardrobe and his writing which seemed to be either a rehearsal or a recital of an article he might easily be writing for a large flat periodical called Vanity Fair, and when he reached its neatly arranged climax she told him that he was far more important than anything even he had written. When she went up to the bedroom which was done in such brilliantly enamelled yellow beds and chairs and dressing-tables and such brilliantly glazed yellow chintz that she always said it had a foreign instead of a domestic finish and that it reminded her of the forehead and the collars of America's most carbolic critic, she opened the little Italian box which she knew was an unsuitable repository for Frederick Thomas's letters. She had been saving them for the correspondence in The Life and Letters of Katharine Faraday, but she was sure they would bring bad luck to the drama of Katharine Faraday and Samuel King, and she burned them in the fireplace under the shining yellow mantel. When she sat down beside Samuel King the next evening at the table Virginia Wise thought was a Duncan Phyfe table, he turned to her half a dozen times to ask her if she liked him, and she began to think that she had finally found the people among whom she was destined to enjoy her small circulation. When he drove her down to Annapolis, she would have been disappointed if he had not held her carefully ungloved hand, and she was entirely truthful when she told him that she had enjoyed seeing him buy a Sheraton bed more than she had enjoyed seeing the Sheraton bed. And when he told his driver that if he felt inclined to turn corners quickly, he must remember how valuable Samuel King was, she was not distressed by an egotism which provided her with such an addition to her repertoire. When he leaned across the Duncan Phyfe table to tell her that her style was like an eighteenth-century marquis's, and that her legs were like an eighteenth-century marquise's, she did not doubt that French women's legs were as thick two hundred years before as they were in nineteen hundred and fourteen. But she told him that she had evidently been wrong in deciding that people born south of Richmond were always polite until they had some good reason for being rude, and that people born north of Richmond were always rude until they had some extraordinarily good reason for being a little less rude. She liked sitting beside another prince of prose on a plumed Heppelwhite sofa, and she would have been disappointed if he had not kissed her as soon as he put down his little amber glass. And she would have been disappointed if he had not told her that although she could certainly provide two sides of a clever conversation instead of one, she would never write a good play as long as she was burdened with her virginity. She thought that his kisses and his conversation were both better suited to red plush than to striped yellow damask, but she did not want to tell him that she did not think she would enjoy being seduced, and she told him that she did not see why she should lie down in a grave decorated only by the white flower of a blameless life and that although she was almost sure she was hopelessly virginal, she would be very much pleased to drive back to New York with him if he could sweep her off her feet, and that she was beginning to feel the weight of her virtue almost as painfully as she had felt the weight of her religion. When she drove into West Forty-fifth Street, she was still shivering from the evening which would have been the scène-à-faire if she had really been playing the third act of the cynical comedy of Katharine Faraday and the celebrated author, and although she thought that her virtue was probably intact only because Samuel King had breathed so noticeably, she had begun to fear that she was really a southern lady and that she would never be swept off her feet. But she was feeling all the satisfaction of a scientific discovery, because she realised how much her future life might be influenced by the knowledge that if a woman tells a man she is hopelessly virginal, he will almost immediately try to prove that she is mistaken.

When she had waited two days for purification from Samuel King's red plush love-making, Katharine Faraday drank three cups of tea and slipped on her orchid satin negligé and powdered her nose and curved her black hair down over her forehead, and then she slipped back into bed and telephoned to David Hofmann. When she saw him through the iron grill of her descending elevator, she liked his hair and his hat and his stick and the cut of his coat. And after she had looked at his grey eyes and listened to his double-stopped voice across a little table in the garden of an Italian restaurant where the high red brick walls and the green vines and the tall green cedars seemed to her an admirable back-drop, she was sure that he was the first man she had ever seen who had a soul, and she was sure that she was in love for the first time. She saw no reason to doubt that he took an interest in the subjects which were discussed and decided again every month in the magazine he edited, and in her second sentence she managed to quote one of the editorials she supposed he had written. And she told him that she had not enjoyed the war except when she was pasting a purple stamp on one of her lavender letters, and that her social and her aesthetic conscience were both unhappy when she stayed with Virginia Wise, because she felt that the butler and the two footmen and the maids were always giving a carefully rehearsed and directed play, and that even though Virginia Wise had learned to lunch in a hat and to dine in a tea-gown, she always seemed to have drifted down to a stage where she was as out of place as flesh and blood actors are in front of Russian scenery. He did not answer her by rehearsing his next editorial, and when he slipped a quotation from Virginal Succession into the sentences in which he became the first eminent author who had insisted on talking about her writing instead of his own, she ceased to regret that Samuel King had wanted to get on to the third act while she wanted to linger in the second half of the first act. She did not think she had found a man whom she would enjoy endorsing by a marriage as public as her mother's ideas of propriety still demanded, but she was sorry that a first meeting cannot be anything more than a prologue unless it is to be a one-act play, and that she felt obliged to wait until she sat down in the same little garden on Friday evening before she could ask him why marriage decreased a man's distinction so abruptly, and why only the perpetuation of a dynasty could make fatherhood dignified. When he told her that pride would not allow the father of a two year old son to admit his own absurdity, and that he supposed even a man's failings were not as well known as he thought them, she was able to smile while she told him that she did not think he should have written to tell her that he admired her style as much as a husband and father could properly admire it, and that she did not think he should have asked her on Wednesday to dine with a man whose wife was displaying his son to her own mother in San Francisco. She did not tell him good-bye when she told him good night, but she was sure she would never let herself see him again. She went on feeling sure while she was looking carefully at the face he had just seen and which he had said was exactly the face which belonged with such a style. But when she lay down with the palms of her hands pressed flat against her legs, she did not mind having him suspect that the name of his son had sent a blazing disappointment down her whole body, and she was almost sure that on Sunday she would sit down and look up at him and then tell him that she was hopelessly virginal. She did sit down on his desk and look up at him when he took her down to his office to see an editorial he thought she might like, and she was sure she was happy for the first time when she found that his interest in her was no more exclusively literary than Frederick Thomas's and Samuel King's. And when her black hair and her orchid georgette were pressed against his remarkably white shirt and his hand had slipped through the long corded slit in her sleeve, she told him how hopelessly virginal she was by telling him that she thought she would like to write a play and have her characters take the responsibility for her American sentences, and that the play would be called No Sheets if he thought it a good title for a play about a girl who could not face the idea of marriage or even of seduction, and whose young man thought she might manage to lose her virtue if the scene were part of the evening instead of being part of the night.

After a month when her first hour in bed was always an hour of rainbow spray, Katharine Faraday felt that she did not care whether any one else thought David Hofmann presentable or unpresentable. And she felt that she had been very young and very inexperienced when she thought that the most satisfactory evenings were the evenings she spent sitting across a table from a man who was not too much more interested in her than she was in him. She also thought that she did not mind David Hofmann's having a wife and son. But when she read in the wide column of the summer's most discussed literary gossiper that he had run into David and Angela Hofmann at a play called He Who Gets Slapped, her whole body burned with the blazing fall of their names. She did not tell him why she was going away, but he understood her well enough to tell her that she was always writing her emotions down in black and white without waiting for either tranquillity or a pencil, and when she had been back at the little hotel in North

Carolina for a week, she was still sure she had never been so unhappy before and she wrote in her notebook that unhappiness is a state where a mind cannot rest happily on either the past or the future, and where it aches from tossing back from the past it cannot look at and back from the future it cannot look at. She was sure that David Hofmann would regret her more and admire her more if she were in a place where he would like to be, and she decided that Paris was the best place to observe comedies of manners, and she persuaded Marian Faraday that Paris might poultice a wound left by the loss of a satisfactory husband and that it was certainly the most economical place to get French frocks and a French accent for a nine year old daughter. She was not sure whether she wrote to David Hofmann again because she was still in love with him or because he was the editor of a magazine for which she might want to write another paper. But she thought she was sure when she saw him walk across the gangway of the Paris, and when she had to leave the little cabin in which he had kissed her and then lifted her up in both his arms to kiss her again.

Although she had a long ticket which entitled her to a first-class seat until the auto bus AL reached the church of the Madeleine, Katharine Faraday left it at the Chamber of Deputies because she could no longer endure sitting behind the embraces of the young Frenchman who wore his black hat exactly like David Hofmann and the French girl who was wearing a purple hat. She walked across the bridge with her hand against the thin white envelope in the pocket of her mole-skin coat, and when she passed a pianist called Paderewski, she did not think of anything except that she must remember to tell David Hofmann about the morning when she was going to have the last fitting of her fuchsia crêpe satin and her coat with the fuchsia feather lining, and when she had met Paderewski in the middle of the Place de la Concorde. She also thought of the play she was writing, and of what David Hofmann would think about the man whose father went from Europe to America just in time for his son to be born in the Promised Land, and who spent his whole life in longing for the continent where he should have been born. She thought that she would call the play Egypt, and then she began to wonder if she had become more important to David Hofmann than his wife, since she was in Egypt and his wife was only in the Promised Land, and what he would think about her when he saw her play, and what he would think about her in the fuchsia crêpe satin if he took her down to his office to see the proofs of another editorial of his or the proofs of the little article called The Fair Land of France which she had just sent to him. She would not let herself go into the bank for her letters until she had walked down the Faubourg Saint Honoré and found fuchsia crêpe and fuchsia feathers a satisfactory approach to black hair and a face the color of a freesia. And when she found a thin white envelope on which her name was miraculously written in David Hofmann's flowing letters, she would not let herself open it because she was going to lunch with a spinster called Catherine Robinson, and she knew that the letter might be one of those letters which had sent her back to the Hotel des Saints Pères and left her lying in her bed for two days and two nights while her fountain rose and fell and dropped its rainbow spray. She did not think that Catherine Robinson enjoyed her own virginity, since she was very attentive to an Angora cat and a Persian cat who could hardly be anything except a purchasable substitute for a husband and a baby, and after she had spent half an hour sitting beside Catherine Robinson on the velvet seat beside the wall in Colombin's restaurant on the Rue Cambon, she did not feel that she could watch her rigid fingers lift another stalk of asparagus or that she could listen to the description of another of the smaller objects in the Cluny Museum or the Carnavalet Museum. She said that she did not like things and that she did not like anything except emotions and ideas, and then she felt obliged to say that she was beginning to think the best way to get rid of her virginity would be to go out and abandon herself with the first chauffeur who did not have a beard, and who probably would not think she was in love with him or that she wanted him to ask her to marry him. But while she was talking of chauffeurs her left hand was touching the blue stamp and the flowing letters on the envelope David Hofmann's long slim fingers had miraculously touched. When she was back in the little room which looked down on the blue hydrangeas in the hotel's little courtyard, she took out the letter which might be a delighted answer to the letter in which she had told him that her boat was due in New York two safe days before the anniversary of the fourth day of June when she had first seen him through the iron grille of an elevator. She had opened the box in which the fuchsia crêpe and its bands of shaded beads were lying in a hundred sheets of tissue paper, and she had ordered the hot bath in which she would read the letter for the third time and the fourth time and the fifth time. But when she took the thin sheets out of the envelope and read on the first page that David Hofmann had just become the father of another son, she felt a sickness worse than the sickness she had felt at the Grand Guignol and she sank down into it while she wondered if she should throw herself down among the hydrangeas or whether she should only throw down the fuchsia crêpe.

When Marian Faraday was unable to consider her sister's sudden distaste for America a reason why she should keep her ten-year-old daughter in a land where she had already discovered that men are not made precisely like women and that all women do not dislike being kissed, Katharine Faraday decided that staying in a town where she had been so unhappy was less bearable than going away from it with a spinster who had rigid fingers and who liked to look at small objects, and she persuaded Catherine Robinson to feel an interest in the modern German theatre which could only be satisfied by a month in Berlin and a month in Salzburg. She knew that she disliked Paris because her own small circulation did not seem to be among Frenchmen or among either the American men or the Englishmen who liked living in Paris, and she knew that she might not have remembered David Hofmann's last kiss so long if she had found an admirer more presentable than the tall fair painter who had wanted to kiss her when she went with him to gather lilies of the valley in the forest of Rambouillet or more presentable than the sunburned Englishman who had not enjoyed the advantage of an Oxford education and who misunderstood a play called Six Characters in Search of an Author so mortifyingly that she told Catherine Robinson she would rather be violated soul and body than accept his protection to another play. Ever since Samuel King had shown his insight into feminine characters by telling her that she did not like women, she had been feeling that a husband would be as useful during a journey over Europe as he would be between eight and twelve on an American evening. But until she had travelled to Berlin and shared a room in the Hotel Bristol with Catherine Robinson, she had not realised the misfortune of being a woman who is too unhappy to endure being alone, and who does not enjoy sharing a room with a woman, and who is sure she would not enjoy sharing it with a man. She remembered the days when she had enjoyed saying that nothing is so immodest as modesty, and she remembered Mrs. Rutherford Cobb when she began to look again at modesty combined with tidiness. After she had vainly tried to admire the style of a book called Fermé la Nuit so much that she would not see the rigid bony fingers with which Catherine Robinson took clean white papers from one of her bags and laid them in the Hotel Bristol's clean drawers, and with which she ran virginally white ribbons through the eyelets of her nainsook nightgowns and her nainsook chemises, and with which she folded the nightgowns and the chemises and laid them on her own clean white paper, Katharine Faraday went into the bathroom which the state of the mark allowed her to have. But she could not enjoy the hottest water she had felt in Europe, and she began to wonder if she would be very much like Catherine Robinson when she was a forty year old virgin instead of a virgin who had just begun to notice the drooping throats of other women and to wonder how much more than thirty-one years they had lived. She also began to wonder how much longer presentable men would offer her even the most dishonourable affection, and she began to think that she would be very careful of the orchid georgette nightgown with the slightly paler lining and the rows of hemstitching which she had seen in a window of the Faubourg Saint Honoré when her hand was touching a satisfactory letter from David Hofmann.

On the twentieth day of June, Katharine Faraday sat down beside Catherine Robinson and asked for vorspeisen and roast goose and kümmel, and then she looked out of the window at the River Elbe, and then she finished talking about the sofas and the tall clocks and the pink and yellow stoves in the royal palace, and she began to talk about the reasons why she was feeling relieved that she had finally seen the Sistine Madonna. Her mind was still tossing back from the unhappy future and back from the unhappy past, but she was able to look back into the less adjacent past and to tell Catherine Robinson that Mrs. Randolph had thought every young lady should read the life and the letters of a bishop called Phillips Brooks, and that ever since she had read it she had wanted to see Raphael's masterpiece so that she could tell all Bostonians and all Episcopalians what she thought about a man who could say that henceforth it would be to all other pictures what the Bible was to all other books. When a tall fair-haired young man with a fair little mustache sat down at the same table with them, she supposed he was another of the tall fair young Saxons who had surprised her by looking like young Goethes and even like Lohengrin, son of Parsifal. She knew that all Germans spoke English, but since she knew that no one born north of Baltimore ever understood anything she said at their first meeting, she did not suppose that even a German would be likely to understand her. When the tall young man laughed in the middle of her conversational plans, she was so pleased by his ability to appreciate her cleverness that she was able to go on talking to him about the Dresden Gallery's misfortune in having nearly all its pictures go out of fashion. When he told her that his name was Alden Ames and that he had been born in the little town which was celebrated by Ralph Waldo Emerson and Louisa May Alcott, she was almost sure he would not be anything worse than economical, and she did not suffer the hot untidy feeling she had supposed she would always suffer when she talked to a man who had not been properly introduced to her. And when he said that he had written a play which was called Holly-hock Minds and which had lasted seven weeks at the Forty-Third Street Theatre, she was sure that she would be able to finish the play which would make David Hofmann understand what he had lost.

After Alden Ames sat between her and Catherine Robinson at a performance of Maria Stuart in which Queen Elizabeth seemed to be dressed after one of Queen Victoria's later portraits, Katharine Faraday was sure that she understood the state of the German theatre. And after he played with her heliotrope sash while the Moscow Kammer Theatre's Phèdre was allowing her to use the intermissions in telling him how much the Phèdre at the Comédie Française had reminded her of the acting in an Uncle Tom's Cabin she had once slipped away from school to see, she was sure that she understood the state of the Russian theatre. And when he played with the long beaded sash of the fuchsia crêpe she had felt able to wear to Tristan and Isolde, and then held her hand all through the second act, she felt that at last she could enjoy hearing the only music in which her rainbow fountain rose and fell, and she was sure that she understood herself at last. When she was lying in his arms on the day-bed in his sitting room, she was wondering if the violet and fuchsia pillows did not mean that he had been expecting her to go back with him, but she was sure that she was about to feel the melting of the hard little core of consciousness she had instead of a soul, and that she was about to feel everything Isolde had ever felt for Tristan. She still wanted to wait until another night, but she could not tell Alden Ames that she did not want what he was trembling with desire to give her, and what seemed to her much more remote than a kiss after he had given it to her.

When Katharine Faraday lay awake all night, she knew that she had not been swept away, but she knew that she was no longer a virgin, and she was not unhappy about the past or about the future in which she would be able to tell David Hofmann that another man had been able to sweep her off her feet and in which she would not tell Alden Ames anything. But when she looked out at the sun rising over the River Elbe, she realised that for two weeks she would have to endure a suspense less bearable than the suspense she would have felt if she had been justly accused of murder, and if a jury had deliberated her fate for something like three hundred and thirty-six hours, and she considered putting on the heliotrope georgette with the beautifully cut circular skirt and the three beautifully flat little collars and going down to throw herself into the wide smooth stream. But she persuaded herself that although she was not afraid of death, she could not endure the idea of having Alden Ames think he had been able to bring her to a situation from which she could only step into another world, and she did not do anything except persuade Catherine Robinson that she wanted to go to Leipzig and see Georg Kaiser's new play about Joan of Arc. She felt as if a figured veil had been dropped over her, and as if she could not see the world or the future except through the pattern on the veil, and she thought of the day when she had read that David Hofmann had become the father of another son and of all the other days when she should have been happy because she had not yet laid herself down among Alden Ames' violet and fuchsia pillows and left herself suffering because she did not know what was happening in her own body, and because she could not control her own body. She wished that she was the hotel porter who carried down her bags and who could never have a baby, and she wished that she was Catherine Robinson who could never have a baby, and she wished that she was either of the nuns who sat across from her in the compartment and who had probably never had any babies. She thought about what she would do if the worst possible thing happened when nothing happened at all, and she discovered that she had been right when she had thought she was not brave enough not to be virtuous. She wrote two acts of her play because she felt obliged to show Alden Ames that she could write a better play than he had written. But she could not look at the name she had written on its first page, and she could not read a book or a paper because all books and all papers mentioned fathers and mothers and sons and daughters, and she could not look at more than one act of Georg Kaiser's play because Joan of Arc was either a virgin or not a virgin, and she could not look at the Thomaskirche because Johann Sebastian Bach had played its organ and she knew that he was the father of twenty children, and she could not stay in any Catholic church because a statue of the Virgin Mary and her son always cut a line of agony from her throat down through her delicate little brown line. After the Sunday morning when she felt a peace she had never imagined after she saw that nature had not asked her to pay anything except two hundred and sixty-four hours of suspense, she still felt that she would never again want a man to admire either her hair or her voice or her writing, and she was sure that if she were ever able to look at a play again, she would want to walk into the theatre and out of the theatre with another woman.

After she had suffered six months of gradually lessening agony with the approach of every new moon, Katharine Faraday began to feel that she would like to go back to Atlanta, and that she would like to prove her cleverness to Alden Ames and to the rest of her world by getting No Sheets produced at a theatre as distinguished as the theatre where Hollyhock Minds had enjoyed seven weeks of performance. She did not think about the moonlit nights when she would be passing Palermo and Monaco and Gibraltar, and she did not think about the presentable or unpresentable man who might lie in the deck chair beside hers and who might make the beauty of phosphorescent nights endurable for her. But when she found herself lying in a long chair beside a tall young clergyman called Silas Stuart, she was able to tell Catherine Robinson that she was touched by the tragedy of a man who believed in the efficacy of his own baptism even though he had been baptized by a very Protestant clergyman, and who had suffered the misfortune of being baptized Silas when he would have liked to be baptized Cuthbert or even Anselm. She was able to say the things she was sure he wanted her to say about the Apologia pro Vita Sua, and she risked being sick long enough to walk down to her cabin and present him with a leaf she had broken from the ivy which was growing over the church John Henry Newman had built at Littlemore. And she was even able to go into the dining-saloon and hear him say mass and find out what kind of sermon could be preached by an American who had enjoyed the advantage of an Oxford education. She was able to endure the ugly folding of the women who knelt down to hear him pray, but when she saw the strangely long head of the boy who was serving his carefully Anglican service, she felt that she could not go on looking at a boy who had so obviously been born. When he began his sermon, she was able to write down a note that stepping out of a service into a sermon is as much like stepping across the footlights as stepping into a dining-room between a carefully rehearsed butler and a carefuly rehearsed footman. But when he said that any one should be able to believe in the virgin birth of Jesus, since any sufficiently sensitive woman could think about the possibility of becoming a mother long enough to prove the theory of parthenogenesis, she was obliged to slip out of the dining-saloon, and even the memory of all the pictures of Saint Catherine's mystic marriage did not keep her from having her chair moved to the glass-enclosed deck above the deck where the Reverend Silas Stuart's chair stood. And when he came up to regret her as a neighbour and to mention the comforts of belief in a firmly established church and a just God and a future life, politeness did not keep her from telling him that beliefs of any kind would certainly ruin her style.

A month after No Sheets had been admired by all the dramatic critics except the two men whose admiration would have pleased her, and after she was sure that she had been able to write a play which would almost certainly last at least a week or two longer than the play Alden Ames had written, Katharine Faraday had the satisfaction of discovering that at last she had been bored by a celebrated man. And on the day after she had discovered that Moonlight had not made her enjoy its author's cockney conversation, she had the satisfaction of consenting to receive the young cousin who had begged Mildred Cobb to take him to see the author of a play he admired as much as he admired Six Characters in Search of an Author—and the satisfaction of consenting with a reluctance just apparent enough not to interfere with politeness. She had begun to feel at last that a peg has at least as much right to be square as a hole has to be round, and she was sure she did not care whether either Alden Ames or David Hofmann agreed with the men who said that she had written a brilliant play, and she was sure Philip Cobb would only be another of the young men who wrote about funerals and football games and legal and illegal executions. But when she was slipping into a fuchsia chiffon frock which was as entirely without sleeves as most of the frocks she had been wearing since she had discovered that the highest curve of a feminine arm apparently has a definite effect on a man who takes either an honourable or a dishonourable interest in her, she opened her notebook before she tied one of the long sashes she had been wearing since she had discovered that men like to play with sashes, and she wrote down her conviction that successful women are the women who learn to take advantage of being women before their throats begin to droop. When her hand first touched Philip Cobb's hand, she remembered the day when Cary Fairfax sat down across from her in the first seat of the first row of desks, and then she remembered the day when he slipped an iron ring around his ear, and she began to think that at last

Georgia was providing another hero for the romance of Katharine Faraday. She was almost sure that some day she would tell Philip Cobb how carefully his head and his long deep-set eyes and his delicately curved nose and his short upper lip had been modelled and how beautifully they had been finished. And when her hand touched his hand again just before he went out behind Mildred Cobb, she was almost sure that some day she would tell him about the way his upper lip closed against his lower lip while he talked of the plays he was going to write some day, and she began to suspect that she might enjoy having him sit at her feet and by her side at the same time. After she had sat beside him during the second act of Tristan and Isolde, she was almost sure that some day her cheek would lie against his deep ivory cheek and that she would curve her hand around his beautifully modelled ear, and that when he had gone she would lie down flat on her face and feel a strange aching, and that the electric spray would fall down her arms and cut a burning exit through the palms of her hands. And when she sat beside him during the second act of Pelléas and Mélisande and saw him holding the very end of her long heliotrope sash, she was almost sure that an evening would come when he would put out his hands to her as blindly as a baby reaching out his hands and his mouth for his mother, but she was sure that he would never look at her and then become damp around his eyes—the eyes she had already told him were like a phosphorescent night on the Mediterranean. She supposed an evening would come when she would tell him that he had tied together enough last straws to make a sheaf of wheat on the grave of their love, and she knew she would not be consoled by the opportunity of using a phrase she admired, and she supposed she would tell him that she had been mistaken when she thought she had found a man who had a soul, and when she had hoped that her small celebrity would take the place of her body. She supposed she might even tell him that she was as glad to be rid of her virginity as she was to be rid of her religion, but that she had never been sure she was hopelessly virginal until the morning when she saw the sun rise over the River Elbe. And she was sure she would tell him that he had shattered her last illusion, but she knew she would go on discovering that one illusion had been left to her a minute before, and that she would discover it every time she heard another illusion shattering on the path behind her.